Gatehaven Chronicles

The Ghost, The Thief and the God-Hammer

Martin Dallard

AuthorHouse™
1663 Liberty Drive
Bloomington, IN 47403
www.authorhouse.com
Phone: 1-800-839-8640

©2010 Martin Dallard. All rights reserved.

No part of this book may be reproduced, stored in a retrieval system, or transmitted by any means without the written permission of the author.

First published by AuthorHouse 3/3/2010

ISBN: 978-1-4490-9147-7 (sc)

Printed in the United States of America
Bloomington, Indiana

This book is printed on acid-free paper.

This book is dedicated to Sally-Anne, whose patience and understanding helped me when staring at a blank page. To Daughty, whose tales of drama from the playground reminded me what it was like to be at school again. To P.B. the best proof reader out there. Also, to Mum, she knows why. And lastly, to Dad, who has waited long enough…

Hope you enjoy! :)

Martin Pellatt 13/4/10

Hope you Enjoy! ☺

FIRST NIGHT

It was midnight before he made his move. He slipped from beneath his bed quilt and regarded his reflection in the mirror on the wardrobe door. The dark grey body suit covered him from his toes up to his neckline. It had taken him six weeks of toil with the sewing needle to get the finished article. He went back to the bed, crouched down and pulled from underneath it his school sports bag.

Delving inside he withdrew the carefully folded items. He put on the dark gloves. Next, he pulled on the mask, fussing with the position of the eyeholes. Then he reached for the cape. He fastened it around his neck with press-studs hidden beneath the cloth.

At last, he was ready for the night! Crossing to the window, he drew back the heavy curtains and opened the catch. A cool breeze washed over him. With the sound of his own heart hammering in his ears, he climbed out onto the windowsill, eyeing the apple tree opposite him.

A flicker of doubt crossed his mind as to the risk he was taking.

"You can do this," he muttered under his mask. He kicked hard away from the sill, his legs propelling him across the gap, fingers claw like, ready to grab the closest branch. At the last second, he felt a tugging from behind. He lost all his forward momentum.

And down he went.

He landed hard; his fall broken by several dustbin bags beneath the tree. His weight split the bags open, spilling their contents onto the patio. The wind was knocked from him and he lay groaning for a moment. Just then, Mum and Dad's bedroom light went on overhead.

"What was that Bob?" he heard his mum say harshly through the partially open window.

"I'll get out and have a quick look." his dad replied.

Casting around for a place to hide, he dived for cover behind the tree just as an oblong of yellow light stabbed its way into the garden.

The upper window opened and Dad poked his head out for a better look. He heard Dad groan and say, "That fox has been giving us a visit again. It's been through the bags. I'd better go and pick it up; I won't have time in the morning."

Foxes! That gave him an idea. If he could distract Dad for just a moment, it might just be possible to slip past him into the house unseen. The outside light went on, flooding the garden with yet more light. The key turned in the lock and the next moment he heard Dad's slippered feet step out onto the patio. He shrank back into the folds of his ebony cape.

His eyes fell on Mum's potting trowel left out on the grass. It was only an arm length away. Now if he could get to it before Dad got to him…

Springing for the trowel, he snatched it up. Turning, he threw the trowel as far away from him as possible. It hit the back fence with a resounding thud.

"Who's there?" Dad spluttered, taken by surprise. He crouched and picked up a heavy broom. Now with a weapon to hand he cautiously picked his way to the back of the garden.

Holding his breath as Dad moved nearer, and finally past him, he crept toward the open patio door. Once inside he threw a quick look over his shoulder to see whether dad had noticed him.

Pausing at the bottom of the stairs to be sure that Mum was still in bed, he slinked up to upper landing, careful not to place his foot on the third step from the top, as it creaked. Once back in his room, he removed the mask and hastily got under the quilt, tucking it under his chin, hiding the costume. He lay there feigning sleep.

Five minutes later, his straining ears heard Dad's heavy tread on the stairs. The footsteps paused for a moment then approached his door. He turned his head just as the door opened. He did not move, but kept his eye on Dad's shadow stretching itself across the wall. Presently the door closed again, taking the light and Dad's shadow with it.

He lay there for a while staring up at the ceiling. What had gone wrong? What would have happened if Dad had found him in the garden? How would he have explained himself? Question after question worried its way out of his tired mind and all of them went unanswered.

"So much for The Grey-Ghost," he whispered up at the ceiling. And with that, the troubled lad knew no more.

1.

THE GATHERING STORM

The night sky rumbled with approaching storm. Darius Crane stood before the large window of his luxurious office suite, looking out at the twinkling lights of London. Lightning lit up the rain-swollen clouds, promising to drench the city below. Thunder boomed high above Crane's steel and glass skyscraper. The building seemed to shudder before the fury that raged overhead.

Just then his intercom beeped, and crossing the vast stretch of carpet to his desk, Mr Crane pressed the flashing red button. "Yes Janice?" he enquired.

"There's a call on your secure line Mr Crane," Crane's personal assistant spoke in a very businesslike voice.

"Put it through would you?"

"One moment Sir," Janice replied, and a moment later, another red button lit up on Crane's panel.

He lifted the phone to his ear. "This is Crane."

"It's Wade," a self-assured voice replied.

"I know," Crane said. "You're the only one who has this number. I'm a busy man, Mr Wade. Would you get to the point?"

"Sir, I've found it."

"Are you certain of that?" Crane asked, barely keeping his voice from shaking.

"Yes Sir, I'd stake my life on it."

"Very well. Have you taken possession of the item yet?"

"No Sir," Wade replied. "The moment has not yet presented itself."

"Where is the item now?" Mr Crane pressed on.

"It's about to be shipped from Norway. I believe it is headed for the History Museum in London. I'll know for certain once I've laid my hands on the shipping manifesto."

"That is unacceptable," Crane said. "I must see to it that it is redirected to the museum in GateHaven."

"Why GateHaven?"

"That need not concern you Mr Wade. Crane said. "Keep me posted; I want to know exactly what is going on. Report anything, no matter how unimportant you may think it to be. Am I making myself clear?"

"As crystal, Sir."

Mr Crane put the phone down and returned to his post at the window. His head was swimming with the news. They had found it. After all those years of fruitless searching, someone else had found it for him.

Thunder boomed overhead again and he raised his eyes to the storm clouds, a secretive smile creasing his face.

2.

SCRAPES AT SCHOOL

Billy Blake yawned as he approached the gates of Prince John's High School on a cloudy Monday morning in early October. There was the usual amount of lacklustre chaos going on in the playground that was customary with the first day after the weekend. Entering the school building Billy made his way through the corridor and past other kids busying themselves in their lockers, getting books for morning classes. Just then a dry voice piped up over the crowd.

"Morning William, have a nice weekend?"

Billy groaned inwardly as Kyle McKinley surrounded by his regular crowd, sauntered towards him. The general rumpus of the morning chaos died away. There was an expectant hush as everyone waited for something to happen.

"Hello Kyle," Billy said, already resigned to the inevitable abuse coming his way.

Although the two of them were in the same year, Billy was short for his age, whereas Kyle was the direct opposite, being as tall as most of the teachers. Billy was fair-haired, blue eyed with a nose full of freckles, and McKinley's hair was dark, with eyes of the deepest brown.

"How's the comic collecting coming along?" McKinley asked in a mock serious tone. "Who's that hero you like so much?"

"Uni-Man," Billy mumbled.

"Right," Kyle replied. "So all is well with the comic universe you live in?"

Billy blinked. "Sorry, don't follow you."

McKinley shrugged, "You don't live in the real world with the rest of us do you? But then I'm not surprised, since you obviously take after your old man. I mean to say he's always stuck in that museum of his isn't he? You're both living in your own fantasy worlds."

"Say what you want about me," Billy took a step forward, "but say anything about my family again and I'll flatten you!"

Kyle's face split in a wide grin. "You know Bill, for a moment there I almost thought you had a backbone."

Without another word, he shouldered his way past Billy, his loyal followers bringing up the rear. Letting out a quiet sigh Billy slouched his way along with the rest of the crowd.

By the time he made it to class everybody else was there, including their form teacher Mr Miller, who looked up from the registration book.

"Ah, there you are Billy, take your seat please." He smiled and motioned with his hand toward the middle row of desks.

Dropping his bag onto the tabletop, Billy slumped into his seat and stared vacantly at the graffiti scratched into the wooden lid.

"Morning Billy," a soft voice beside him said, and he turned to look into the face of Jenny Tate, his desk mate at registration.

"Hiya Jen. Sorry, didn't see you there."

Jenny, a pretty thirteen year old with shoulder length blonde hair and green eyes leaned closer to Billy.

"You're quiet this morning, anything wrong?"

Billy sighed. "I'll give you three guesses," he said and jerked his thumb over his shoulder.

Swivelling in her chair, Jenny looked toward the back of the room. There was McKinley sat in the back row of desks flanked on either side by his cronies.

"Pay no attention, you're better than him." She reached over and patted Billy's arm.

Billy kept his eyes lowered to the desk. "I don't know so much," he replied slowly.

"What do you mean?" Jenny asked, frowning.

"Maybe he's right, what he's saying about me."

"I don't understand."

"Well take a look at him," Billy said sullenly. "Then take a look at me. He's got to be one of the most popular kids in the school, and all I seem to do is live for comics and video games."

Jenny was about to reply when Mr Miller called out from the front of the class.

"Okay, now as you all know, tomorrow is the field trip to the museum, so remember to arrive at the school fifteen minutes earlier than normal. Is everyone clear about that?" The only person in the room paying no attention was Kyle McKinley.

"Everything all right at the back Kyle? You don't seem that enthusiastic about the trip."

Kyle put his hand to his mouth and stifled a mock yawn. "Can't wait for it, Sir."

Ignoring Kyle's reply, Mr Miller continued. "As you all know, the new World War II exhibition opens this week, and with it the somewhat controversial display about a band of freedom fighters some say didn't actually exist. I am of course referring to The British Battalion."

There were a few excited murmurs around the classroom. A girl at the back of the class raised her hand into the air.

"Yes Angela?"

"Sir, I still don't understand. Just who was the British

Battalion?"

"I think that Miss Beechum your history teacher will want to answer that one," Mr Miller said with a smile.

"They were supposed to be superheroes or something during the war," a heavily pimpled lad called Dave Thomas said over his shoulder to Angela Bennett.

"Like in the comics?" Angela said quizzically.

"Something like that," Mr Miller said.

"Oh, come on Sir," McKinley's sarcastic voice rang from the back of the class. "Who's going to believe that a group of super powered people were running around fighting Hitler during World War II?"

"Everyone is entitled to their opinion Kyle," Mr Miller said, "and you will have the opportunity to air yours tomorrow. I only wish that I was going with you," he added wistfully.

"Anything for a day off school, eh Sir?" another voice from the back shouted. Mr Miller smiled despite himself. Just then the bell for morning lessons rang.

"Right, everyone off to class," Mr Miller said over the scraping of chair legs as they all rose from their seats. "I'll be seeing some of you after lunch for P.E," he added as they all filed out of the classroom.

Billy riffled through his bag, checking he had the right books for that morning, while Jen lingered next to him.

"Move along you two," Mr Miller urged.

"Sorry Sir," Jen replied. "We'll get out of your way."

"I'd have expected you to be the first out the door, Billy," Mr Miller said.

"Why?" Billy asked.

"Your first lesson's History isn't it?"

It was like someone had switched a light on in Billy's head. His foul mood forgotten, Billy was galvanized into action.

"C'mon, let's go," he said with urgency in his voice, and the next moment was out the door and racing down the corridor, Jen running to catch up.

Two minutes later, the two of them were sitting in the front row of History room A/. The classroom was already buzzing expectantly as Miss Beechum entered the room with a smile on her round face and an armful of photocopied pamphlets.

"Morning class, looking forward to the field trip tomorrow?" She asked cheerily as she put the papers on the desk and straightened her hand knitted cardigan. Clapping her hands to draw everyone's attention, she cleared her throat.

"As you all know, tomorrow is the trip to the museum. The Battalion exhibition is with us for two weeks only before it moves back to London, so I imagine that the museum is going to be busy. It's going to be a fascinating experience for all of us," she went on. "Whether these freedom fighters actually existed has practically been proven beyond doubt, yet there are still some who believe the whole thing to have been merely propaganda to boost morale during the dark days of World War II.

"Were they nothing more than urban legends? Or were they indeed government agents, their fantastic powers the results of secret experiments to produce an army of indestructible soldiers? But for today's lesson, we will concentrate on the Battle of Britain and the effect this crucial fight was to have on the rest of the war."

The rest of the lesson was pretty vague to Billy. Jen would occasionally dig him in the side with her elbow to snap him out of it, and for a minute or two it would work. But then he would lapse back again. For Billy Blake, Tuesday morning couldn't arrive soon enough.

3.

A NIGHT ON THE TOWN

It had taken him ten minutes to cycle from home to the main part of town. The night sky was cloudless and the stars winked down as he turned off Bridge Street and up a quieter side road. Satisfied that no one had seen him, he dismounted his bike and pushed it into the shadows between two empty shops. He propped the bike against a large wheelie bin, and began to remove his outer clothes.

Beneath was the tight body suit. Removing a black bag strapped to the back of the bike, he unzipped it, and took out his mask, gloves and shoe coverings. He slipped the mask and gloves on, then the elasticised boots. These hid his trainers, making them the same colour as the rest of the suit.

He removed the last item from the bag and clipped it onto his belt. Placing his street clothes into the bag, he zipped it shut. The bag and the bike were hidden behind the wheelie bin.

He set off, running further up the side alley between the darkened shops. The alley he had ducked into was a dead end, yet as a blind brick wall eight feet in height loomed ever closer, he poured the speed on.

At the last moment, he leapt at the wall, driving his foot against it and kicking off. His momentum, combined with his outstretched hands enabled him to grab the top of the wall. With hardly any effort, he pulled himself up onto the top. He set off at a crouch, watching his footing as he went. The wall ended when it met the building nearest to it. Grey-Ghost leapt up and grasped the edge of the low roof, hauling himself up.

He raced across the roof for the fire escape ladder that led to the main roof above him, and moments later, he found himself high above Bridge Street. He had mapped out the rooftops around the city centre, so he knew what was easily accessible without the aid of a rope and grappling hook. That was part of the equipment he was still working on. For now, he would concentrate on his climbing techniques.

Grey-Ghost reached for his belt and unclipped what looked like a radio. He pressed a button and it squealed into life, squawking with static interference. He swore to himself and turned the volume down so that it was a barely audible hiss.

He sat down on the gravelled roof, twiddling with the tuner until he got a better reception. Voices could be heard occasionally, interrupted by more static. They were talking about locations and people. This was a police scanner. Ghost had been listening to it at home earlier, and he knew the police were on the lookout for two lads who were known car thieves.

They had been spotted earlier in the evening lurking around by the Park. That area was poorly lit, perfect cover for someone out to find himself a new car going cheap. He pulled back his glove and looked at his watch. The luminous face told him it was eight thirty. He had to be home by ten; otherwise, Dad would come out looking for him.

He would have to check the park out for himself. He got to his feet, turned the scanner off and returned it to his belt. The roofs were flat, and with the majority of the buildings close by one another, there was no real break in his pace. Ten minutes later, Ghost was looking out over the park from his perch on the roof of the ice cream shop.

He was pleased with his progress. The costume was working fine, without any kind of a hindrance to him. He had scrapped the cape after realising that it was the reason he had fallen from the tree after being snagged on one of the branches. Capes looked cool but really weren't all that practical.

Ghost took another glance at his watch. It was almost nine. If nothing happened within the next twenty minutes, he would have to start making his way back to his bike in order to get home on time.

Just then, a police car rolled on by. It cruised along

the street, slowing every now and then to check out the gloomier spots. Ghost craned his neck, watching the rear lights of the car slowly make their way up the road and finally turn into Larch Drive and out of sight.

He sighed to himself. This line of work was going to involve a lot of patience, and that was something he was going to have to cultivate. Just then, out of the corner of his eye, he spotted movement by the main entrance to the park. It was them!

He scrambled to the edge of the roof. The police scanner had given the Ghost their names. One of them he actually knew.

Bernie Malin. A nasty piece of work if ever there was one. He had always been in trouble, always on report for one thing or another before finally being expelled in his final year. Now it looked as though he had moved on to bigger things.

The lads strolled casually along the street, close to the parked cars that lined the way. Ghost could not really see what they were doing. He needed to get closer.

Ghost raced over to the rear of the roof, scrambled over

its ledge and shimmied down the drainpipe. He picked his way around to the front, keeping to the shadows. Crouching low, he ran from his side of the street over to theirs and through the gate into the park they had just come from. All he had to do now was follow them, but on this side of the wall that separated the park from the street.

His heart was racing as he approached them silently. He drew closer and could hear them talking in low voices.

"This looks like a good one," One voice whispered harshly.

"Check it out," Returned the other. "I'll keep a look out."

Ghost inched ever closer until he could see their heads through the bushes. Thankfully, the foliage was far enough apart for him to make his way to the wall. He peered over, and almost let out a yell of surprise. They were right in front of him. Bernie was the closest, his back to the wall, and he was looking left to right, taking in everything that was going on in the street. The other lad was bent close to a car next to the kerb. It looked like he had something forced down between the window and the door skin itself. A moment later, there was a click.

"Bingo," Bernie said as his partner in crime withdrew a sort of metal scoop from out of the door skin and tucked it back inside his jacket.

He watched as Bernie and his friend scrambled through the sprung passenger door, Bernie settling into the driver's seat. He reached underneath the dashboard and seemed to be rummaging around for something. He withdrew a handful of wires and began sorting through them. He was going to hotwire the car to get it started. Seconds later the car roared into life.

It was now or never. Ghost grasped the top of the wall and vaulted over it, landing right next to the car.

"H-hold it," he said in a quavering voice, his whole body shaking with both excitement and fear. "Get out of the car."

Bernie and friend stared dumbstruck for a moment, hardly believing what they were seeing. And then the moment had passed. Grey-Ghost realised he had lost the element of surprise as Bernie grinned at him through the windscreen.

Now it was his turn to be dumbstruck.

The car thieves made their move. The lad in the passenger seat suddenly swung the door open, hitting Ghost and knocking him off his feet. He sprawled to the pavement, stunned. The car screeched off, the sounds of laughter ringing from inside it. All he could do was watch as the car fishtailed up the road and out of sight.

After finally coming to his senses, Ghost returned to the roofs. He removed the mask and looked at it. If his friends knew what he was doing, they would say he was crazy. He didn't fully understand why he was doing this himself. He had always fantasized about being a hero, battling evil and saving the day. Every kid did. Yet as they grew, so they left their childhood dreams behind. So why hadn't he?

He had been more scared than he ever had in his life before. The climbing, the acrobatics were easy to him. He knew what he was doing. However, coming up against other people was a completely different thing.

Even with his martial arts training, it was possible that he could get hurt, or worse. He tucked the mask into his belt and set off back across rooftops, retracing his steps. As he went, he mulled over the night's events.

There was a knot of disgust growing in his stomach. He should have struck while he still had the element of surprise, he told himself as he vaulted over a ledge and grabbed a metal drainpipe, sliding its length to the quiet alley below. Within minutes he was safely back at the bike, costume hidden beneath his street clothes, the rest of his equipment tucked into the bag. Soon he was pedalling his way home, his mood darker than the night sky above him.

4.

MIX UP AT THE MUSEUM

Tuesday started under a bank of heavy clouds, yet even this could not dampen Billy's enthusiasm. After hastily grabbing a piece of toast for his breakfast, he was out of the front door and heading for Jen's

They discussed the exhibition on their way to school. When they arrived, most of the class was already outside the school chatting idly amongst themselves. Just then, a coach turned the corner and made its way up the road, braking to a halt outside the gates. With a hiss of air, the door swung open and out stepped Miss Beechum looking more excited than Billy had ever seen her.

"Good morning class," she said with a wide smile.

"Are we all here yet?" She took a quick head count. "All present and correct, so let's get going. Every body on board please," she gestured toward the coach.

Billy boarded the coach behind Jen. He noticed that Mr Lamb the fourth year English teacher was seated on the coach. A well-dressed smiling man of sixty, Mr Lamb nodded at the class as they boarded. He was obviously here to assist Miss Beechum today. They seated themselves about halfway along the aisle. Kyle McKinley and company swept on past toward the backseat of the coach. Billy looked the other way.

Twenty-five minutes later they were heading down the tree lined Victoria Promenade, leading directly to GateHaven Museum of Natural History. The coach swung off the main road and pulled to a stop in the coach park at the rear of the building.

The teachers stepped from the coach and waited. One by one, the classmates rose from their seats and filed outside. Mr Lamb was ticking names off on a register. They all congregated on the sweeping steps that led up to the large oak and glass doors of the museum.

"We have a lot to fit in today," Miss Beechum began briskly, "so pay attention. The museum itself does not open until ten this morning." There were groans from the class. "However, as you all know, Billy's Father is Curator here and has graciously invited us to have a look at the exhibition before the rest of the museum opens to the public."

There was a muttering of approval from the kids.

"It's now nine o'clock," Miss Beechum said consulting her watch. "Okay, if you'd all follow me up to the main doors."

As they reached the top, they could hear the bolts on the doors being drawn back. Mr Blake stepped out to greet them.

Good morning," he said cheerily. "You're right on time. Let's get this show started, shall we?"

The class followed him, assembling beneath the vaulted ceiling of the Museum's concourse. The centre of the room was taken up by a reception desk, on which sat a number of pamphlets describing the goings on of the museum, maps depicting the outlay of the various floors and general information needed to navigate the labyrinthine corridors and the many displays on show.

Suspended on cables twenty feet above the reception desk was the blackened skeleton of a vast prehistoric bird that went by the name of Pteradon. Its huge wings were outstretched, and it was as if the ancient reptile had spotted prey and was swooping in for the kill.

"Right then," Mr Blake said clapping his hands together, "this morning you are privileged to be the first ones to see what could easily be the most controversial display of the last sixty years. So if you'll all follow me."

The class filed after Billy's Dad as he wound them through several halls. They passed display cabinets full with fossils and bones of animals long since extinct. Passing beneath the legs of a full-scale tyrannosaurus rex model that stretched across the carpeted aisle, they made their way along a corridor that ended in a large set of double doors. Beyond was a darkened corridor. This swiftly turned a corner that opened out into a scene that astounded them.

It was like stepping back in time. A city scene stretched

out before them, set in the time of the Second World War. The street was pock marked with craters; rubble from damaged buildings littered the roadway.

What windows remained in the surrounding buildings was criss-crossed with tape. The class stood behind a glass barrier separating them from the scene of carnage. Just then, the whole scenario came to life. An air raid siren started wailing; explosions were heard in the distance, and the drone of many planes flying overhead. Suddenly, a woman rounded the corner of a ruined shop. She was wearing a thick woolly coat and a headscarf and she was pushing an old style baby's pram. She was in an obvious hurry yet her progress was slowed by the state of the path. The pram wheels suddenly became stuck and it tipped over onto its side, sending the woman sprawling to the ground. Cries of panic came from the baby, and she scrambled to her feet wrestling the pram back onto its wheels.

So busy was she checking her baby for injuries that she did not notice the wall behind her leaning over at a precarious angle. The bombing had weakened the structure and it was ready to fall.

Looking up, she threw herself across the pram, trying to shield her baby from the impact. The whole class, Miss Beechum and Mr Lamb included, held their collective breath.

He came from nowhere. Miraculously the wall had stopped falling, held in place by a man dressed in army fatigues, his face hidden by a mask. His gloved hands crunched into the brickwork as he actually began pushing the wall back upright. The woman got the pram clear and the next instant the masked man let the brick wall crash to the street.

The woman went over to the mystery man, who was patting dust off his hands.

"You saved us," she said in-between sobs of gratitude. "Who are you?"

"I'm Sergeant Strong, Miss," and he pointed to three stripes on his arm. "You really should get to an air raid shelter. Take care now." Without so much as a backward glance, he leapt up onto the roof of the building opposite and was lost in the darkness.

The whole scene went dark, and red velvet curtains swished together closing the war torn street off from the real world. The class clapped and whistled. Behind the curtain, Billy could hear movement and pneumatic hisses. He surmised the scene was resetting itself ready for the next lot of visitors.

"What you have just witnessed," Miles Blake said when the cheering had stopped, "was the re-enactment of what is said to be the first appearance of a handful of "Special" operatives in the armed forces during the period of World War II. However, did these characters really exist? Or were they just the imagination of someone's over fertile mind?" He gestured for them to follow and he led the way through an arch that opened into a large gallery.

The room was full of display cabinets, all of which contained strange things. There were cases that housed faded documents with "TOP SECRET" stamped across the top in bold red ink.

The class took it in turns to peer through the glass at papers, trying to read the fading ink.

"These documents in the casements before you," Mr Blake said, "are government papers, previously kept secret under the seal of the official secrets act. From all the documentation that has come under the spotlight, it would seem that top scientists working together with the British Government wanted to give the people something to rally behind when we entered the war in nineteen thirty nine. A sort of "mascot" for want of a better word. This mascot would go on to spearhead the fight against the enemy."

"So how come we haven't heard of them?" a disbelieving voice rang from among the sea of faces. McKinley stood there with a sarcastic smirk stretched across his face.

"That's a very good question," Mr Blake said. "Do you know the story of Frankenstein?" Many of the kids nodded. "Well, with information gleaned from certain documents, it would appear that the government were fearful of a backlash. What if the public thought they had created monsters?

"Hence the reason the Battalion became a closely guarded secret by the Home Office. There were sightings of miraculous happenings right through wartime. The scene you just witnessed is a re-enactment of an event that happened in nineteen forty."

"Don't you mean allegedly happened?" Kyle asked again.

"Good point," Mr Blake replied. "We only have the word of the woman saved by the super sergeant to go by. There are many stories similar to this one documented. Soldiers on the battlefield claim to have seen these fantastically powered beings fighting shoulder to shoulder with them."

He paused again then went on, "What I suggest you do now is have a good look around at the many things on display and try to draw your own conclusions. We'll meet up in an hour's time when I'll try to answer any questions you might have."

The group of kids split up. Billy meandered his way through the display cabinets. Against one wall was a glass case taller than Billy's Dad was. Inside it was the tattered remains of a costume draped over a mannequin. Parts of it looked singed in places as though whoever had worn it had been involved in a fire. The material was jet black, but it wasn't like any material he'd seen before. Nothing seemed to be reflecting off the cloth. Below the suit was a description of the exhibit.

THE WRAITH

Little is known of this government agent except that he operated between 1940 and 1948 fighting for the freedom of the people of Great Britain. His identity remains a mystery to this day. There are many stories about his courage and heroism during The Blitz, his displays of great physical strength and speed. Yet the strangest thing known about this man in black was his uncanny ability to be in the right place at the right time when needed most. Then he would vanish as if he was never there. No one heard him speak, no one heard him approach, and no one ever saw him vanish. A true mystery man, if he was ever a man at all. It has been said that he was harder to catch than smoke…

Billy lingered for another minute re-reading the sign then slowly moved on. He picked his way between cabinets, peering in at officially stamped documents under glass. "TOP SECRET: FOR YOUR EYES ONLY." were stamped in big red letters across them. A lot of them were yellowing with age yet they were still readable. A lot of it went over Billy's head. He didn't understand what he was reading for most of it. Only certain things stood out, like; "suitable recipient acquired," "energy transference successful," and "test subject capable of outrunning a motorcycle."

Billy was about to move onto the next aisle, when a heavy hand clamped down on his shoulder. He spun around, only to find himself looking at McKinley.

"What do you want?" Billy said sullenly, shrugging the hand off him.

"Don't be like that," Kyle said, pretending to be hurt. "I only came to ask what you thought about it all." He grinned down at the smaller boy.

"What do you care?" Billy muttered, turning to move on.

"Well I wouldn't want you to cry too hard when you find out all this is fake," McKinley sneered.

"What makes you say that?"

"Just look at it," Kyle said stepping closer. "All you've got here is a bunch of mouldy paper work and a few scraps of cloth. Now I don't know about you but that is hardly concrete evidence. This has been cooked up by ***certain*** people to try to get people to visit these mouldering museums."

Kyle's sneering face cast a look at Mr Blake who was helping some girls with their questions in the opposite aisle.

Billy followed his gaze. "Are you trying to say that my Dad faked all this?"

Kyle grinned. "Museums must really struggle nowadays to make ends meet. What with all the brilliant documentaries on the telly, and with the internet providing all the information anyone really needs, why bother to come to this festering rat trap?"

Billy rushed forward and caught Kyle with an uppercut to the jaw. McKinley went sprawling into his companions, and four of them ended up in a tangled heap on the tiled floor.

McKinley began to climb to his feet, shock written

across his face. It took him a second or two to regain his composure.

"Bet you feel pretty brave with the old man around, don't you? Care to take another swing after school tonight?"

"Name the time and place," Billy spat, eyes blazing.

However, Kyle never got the chance, for at that moment Mr Lamb came charging down the aisle.

"What is going on here?" he thundered, stepping in among the crowd of kids gathering to see for themselves what was happening.

"It's okay Mr Lamb," Kyle said before anybody else could say anything. "Billy and I were sort of re-enacting the Sergeant Strong thing and I sort of tripped over. It's no big deal," he shrugged, patting dust off his trousers, "is it Billy?" he added, looking Billy hard in the eye.

'That's right Sir," Billy went on quickly. "We just got a bit carried away. Sorry."

"We'll be more careful in future," Kyle said, flashing Mr Lamb his fullest smile.

"You'll be in detention, Mr McKinley," retorted Mr

Lamb sharply. "You may well be the best sportsman this school has seen for many a year, but that cuts no ice with me. Now I suggest you all go about your projects before I change my mind and send you all back to the coach."

Slowly, the class divided and went their separate ways again. McKinley looked over his shoulder at Billy and winked.

"Later," he mouthed with a grin.

Billy stooped to pick up the bag he had dropped. Gathering his belongings together, something on the floor caught his eye. He scooped it up. Wide eyed, he pocketed his find as he saw his dad approaching

"What was all that about?" Mr Blake enquired his face grave.

"It's all right Dad," Billy tried to say reassuringly, though his thoughts were on the contents of his blazer pocket. "I'll tell you all about it later." Billy slipped away. What he didn't need right now was for McKinley's gang to see him discussing the tussle with his dad. It was bound to cause more trouble for him.

Oddly, though, Billy didn't really care. It had felt

good to stick up for himself for once. He glanced down at his right hand. The knuckles were starting to sting. That was the first time he had ever hit anyone intentionally.

"That was some punch," a quiet voice behind him said.

Billy turned and looked into Jen's face, grinning.

"How's the hand?" she enquired taking it in her own and inspecting the grazes.

"It's okay," he said, face flushing. He felt a little awkward with Jenny holding his hand like that, yet he didn't pull away.

"He'll think twice before giving you any hassle now," Jen said. She gave Billy's hand a quick squeeze then released it.

There was a sudden commotion at the end of the hall. Shouting and the sound of running feet echoed through the exhibit as the rest of the class made a dash to see what was going on. Billy and Jen followed the crowd at a run.

By the time they made it to the end, there was already a bottleneck of kids straining to see over one another as to what was causing the commotion. Billy could hear Mr

Lamb and his Dad asking for space, and the throng of school kids pushed back. Jen was bouncing up and down on the balls of her feet, trying to see over the heads in front.

Finally losing patience, Jen tapped the shoulder of the girl in front of her. "Can you see what's going on?" she asked, still bobbing up and down.

Becky Thompson turned her head to look at Jenny. Her eyes were full of tears.

"It's..." she began, but her eyes flickered over to Billy and she went quiet.

"It's what?" Billy and Jen asked together, impatiently.

"It's Kyle. He's collapsed. Someone said he's stopped breathing."

5.

PIECE OF THE PUZZLE

The phone rang as the meeting was coming to an end. Darius Crane reached for the receiver, as other men and women in the room fell silent.

"Yes Janice?" Mr Crane enquired.

"Your secure line Sir."

"Would you ask him to hold the line for a minute while I wrap up here?"

"Very good Sir," Janice replied.

Crane replaced the receiver and looked up at the people sat around the oval mahogany table. All eyes were on him, but then they always were.

"My apologies but something has arisen that requires

my immediate attention. I think it will be better if we continue this meeting, shall we say..." Crane glanced at his Omega wrist watch, "...two o'clock this afternoon?"

All heads nodded in agreement. There was no use in arguing the point.

"Thank you Ladies and Gentlemen that will be all."

Crane watched the last of them rise and leave through the double doors. He lifted the phone once more. "Put him through would you my dear," he said smoothly.

There was a pause then a voice spoke. "Mr Crane?"

"Ah, Mr Wade, some good news I hope."

"I'll be retrieving the item for you this morning."

"This morning? Isn't that asking to be caught?"

"Relax Mr Crane; I'm an old hand at this sort of thing. I'll bring the piece to your main office in London tonight. Is midnight too late for you?"

"That would be fine Mr Wade. I'll meet you on the roof."

"The roof?"

"I wouldn't have thought that a man in your line of work would have any problems accessing the roof."

"Very well Mr Crane," Wade said. "Midnight it is."

Crane put the phone down. He rose and crossed the room to a door at the far end. It was featureless, having no handle with which to open it. On the wall beside it was a metal plate. Mr Crane placed a well manicured hand to it. The door swung silently open. The room beyond was for Crane's eyes alone.

One wall was taken up by a vast bookcase, which rose from floor to ceiling. Books of all shapes and sizes cluttered its shelves, ranging in subjects from Viking mythology to black magic. Tomes on werewolves and vampires were scattered among volumes about witchcraft and the fact and fiction regarding Stone Henge.

Crane made for an ornate spiral staircase in the far corner. The room at the top was small, the floor being tiled, with an expensive marble that was highly polished. On pedestals dotted around the place like playing pieces on an oversized chessboard, sat various sized display cabinets.

These contained pieces of armour in various states of repair. There were helmets that were badly dented, some with splits in them. Several swords lay among the collection, all broken and rusted as though they had spent many years in the ground.

In the centre of the room stood a stone plinth. On top of it was another metal plate. Crane walked over and pressed it, stepping back, as a whole section of the floor with the plinth atop it began to rise up with a pneumatic hiss. Within moments Crane was standing before a glass casing, banded with rings of titanium steel.

Sitting inside the case on a purpose built display stand was a glove that looked to be made of cracked leather. The casing didn't seem to have any door to it, and no seams were visible to the naked eye.

A metallic voice spoke harshly. "IDENTIFY," it said without a trace of human emotion.

"Crane, Alpha-27," He answered without hesitation. The front of the casing slid back into the floor.

Crane took a step forward and reached for the glove. It was bigger than his own hand. He flexed his fingers into its tips. It looked like it could fall apart at any moment; it was so tattered and worn. The glove reached almost up to his shoulder. The hide was warm to the touch. There were no seams of any kind, no way to tell how it had been sewn together. Only the knuckles gave any impression of it being made by man, as large rivet-like heads topped them.

Crane cast his mind back to the day he found it, lost in the snowy mountains of Norway. He smiled. It was the first piece of the puzzle he needed to achieve his goal.

And soon he would have the second part. For him, midnight could not arrive soon enough.

6.

THE SNEAK THIEF & THE SPIDER

"Give me room," yelled Mr Blake over the confusion that surrounded him.

"Somebody go out to the main desk," Mr Lamb shouted, "and get them to phone for an ambulance."

However, at that moment, Kyle stirred slowly. "What's going on?" he asked his voice slurred. He started to rise but Mr Blake placed a restraining hand on his shoulder.

"How are you?" Miles asked in a soothing tone. "What happened?"

"We were in the hall outside." McKinley looked up and saw it was Steele talking. "We poked our heads around the door of the nearest room to see what was in there, and the next thing, Kyle's out like a bleedin' light. Me and Talbot dragged him back in here."

Miss Beechum tutted. "That was a silly thing to do. He could have been hurt and you moving him could have made matters worse."

"Sorry Miss," Steele said, "wasn't thinking."

"Obviously," Said Mr Lamb. "I still think it would be a good idea to take him to casualty and get him checked out."

McKinley sat bolt upright, taking Mr Blake by surprise. "I'm fine," he said in a hurry. "I've had worse in a Rugby scrum."

"It's got nothing to do with that little scuffle a few minutes ago has it?" Mr Lamb enquired.

"No!" McKinley barked. "I think I tripped and went into the door frame. Yes, that was it, wasn't it Steele?" He looked hard at Steele making a point.

"Er, yeah," Steele nodded, "that was it."

"And you're sure you feel all right Kyle?" Miss Beechum asked.

"I'm okay. Honest." And with that, McKinley rose to his feet. Mr Blake steadied him as he got up.

"The restaurant will be opening just about now," Mr Blake said. "I think it would be a good idea if you came along with me and we got you a strong cup of tea." He took McKinley by the arm and began steering him out of the room.

Mr Lamb addressed the rest of the class. "I believe you lot have a questionnaire to fill out."

Miss Beechum stepped forward. "Okay, if you can pass these out among you, find yourself a quiet spot and answer the ten questions set out on the paper. Try to make them more than one word answers will you?" she said. "Save a sheet for Mr McKinley, he can do his while he's having his tea."

With lunch finished and the questionnaire out of the way, the kids were free to spend their remaining time looking around the rest of the museum. Jen had gone off with a couple of her friends to look at an exhibition on fashion through the ages. Billy had gone in the opposite direction to the Viking exhibit in Hall Two.

Toward the centre of the room stood a display cabinet that housed a mannequin dressed in reproduction armour of the period, giving an example of what a marauding Viking must have looked like. Beside it was a long cabinet with genuine clothing in it. There were the remains of boots and belts that had somehow survived all this time.

However, one item caught his eye.

It was a belt, and so good was its condition that it looked as though it had been made last week. The belt was thick and looked like it belonged on an Olympic weightlifter. It was fashioned from dark leather with what looked like lambs wool for padding on its inner side. It was riveted at set intervals around its length. Upon the belt buckle was a very fine engraving of a hammer with a particularly large head.

The buckle itself looked as though it was made of a mixture of gold and silver. As the overhead lights reflected off it, so it shimmered with a mixture of colours. It was the coolest belt Billy had ever seen. His eyes drifted to a sign just below the belt itself. It read:

"The engraving on the buckle represents the Hammer of Thor, the God of Thunder, whom the Vikings worshipped. It is possible that the belt was a token offering to the Gods, allowing its owner passage into Valhalla. Time has had little if no effect on the belt, and remains untarnished, being in as fine a state of condition as when it was first made all those centuries ago."

Billy remained a few minutes longer admiring the belt before moving on. He knew that the famed "Sapphire Spider" was on display, so he figured that he would have a quick look. He joined back up with a few stragglers and together they made their way to the Central Hall.

This hall was the largest, rising almost sixty feet into the air and topped off by a glass dome. There was a guided tour underway.

"And here we have the fabled "Sapphire Spider," the guide was saying. "It belongs to Sheikh Aziz Mohammed Ibun Khan and is on generous loan to us for a limited time. As you can see, The Spider's body is four inches long with a leg span of nearly nine inches. The body and legs made out of gold. Each of the eight legs has eight sapphires set into it, making sixty-four sapphires in total. To finish off, the Spider sits in a web made of pure silver."

"The eyes are red," a Japanese woman among the audience said in very good English. "What stones are they?"

"The eyes are rubies, all eight of them," the guide replied with a smile.

"How much is the Spider worth?" another voice among the crowd asked.

"The Spider is priceless."

The crowd murmured appreciatively. Personally, Billy couldn't see what all the fuss was about. Another question was asked by a voice he recognised only too well.

"What sort of security system does this museum have in displaying something so expensive?" Kyle McKinley asked.

"If you would take a look at the tiny holes that circle the Spider in the ceiling overhead," the guide said, and all eyes followed her pointing finger, "those are the apertures for the computerised laser grid system which envelope the Spider in a net of light. If broken it trips a silent alarm at GateHaven Police Station, as well as setting off numerous internal alarms in the building and every exit to this hall will automatically close with bullet-proof and ram proof steel reinforced doors. As well as the security doors there is the release of a sedative through the ventilation system in the hall which I have been told will incapacitate anybody in these rooms within a minute of being breathed in."

"Could you repeat that in English?" an elderly man in a cloth cap and overcoat said. The others laughed.

"Knockout gas," the guide grinned. "It floods the room and puts anybody to sleep for hours." She then pointed to the floor. "At night when the museum is closed, the weight sensitive floor tiles are activated. Anything weighing heavier than a mouse will once again set off all the defensive systems. The museum is impossible to break into at night. It has a twenty strong security force patrolling its corridors and perimeters, over one hundred cameras scan the halls, all hidden of course," she added as she saw heads turn to locate the cameras mentioned.

"Even the roof of this building is alarmed."

"It sounds like this place is even harder to break into at night," The old man said with a sound like awe in his voice.

"That's right," the guide said proudly. "You'd have an easier time of it trying to steal the Crown Jewels."

"Then I guess I'd better do it now."

Before anyone could move, the pensioner threw a small black disc onto the floor. There followed a bang and a large flash. Everyone yelled, blinded by the blast of intense light, and they stumbled into one another, unable to see a thing.

The old man surged forward onto the podium. As he lifted the Spider off its stand, there was a blast of gas directed at his face. It did not seem to have any effect on him at all, as he pocketed the Spider and started racing for the door.

The escape proof doors were already sliding down into place to seal the room. Billy had thrown himself to the floor to get away from the gas billowing out of the podium. People were falling to the floor, legs no longer able to support them.

The only reason Billy was still awake was the fact that he had held his breath the moment the gas jets hissed. He crawled away on his hands and knees. It was no use; he couldn't fight it any longer. Billy's lungs exploded as he breathed out. At once, he tasted the sickly sweet gas in his mouth.

The fog was so thick now that he could only just make out dim shapes of people lying on the ground. From somewhere far off he heard a grinding noise like something straining as if about to break. There was a sudden gust of wind. Billy raised his drooping head to locate where the sound was coming from. What he saw made him smile, for the gas must have been making him see things. Then everything went black.

7.

INSPECTOR MCKINLEY INVESTIGATES

Inspector McKinley and Detective Sergeant Harrison screeched to a halt outside the museum. There were already police cars there as well as several ambulances. McKinley got out, his face grey as he approached the nearest ambulance first.

"Who's in the back?" McKinley asked suddenly, trying to mask his urgency.

"Couple of tourists," the paramedic replied. "Reaction to the gas. It was only concentrated in the one hall so the rest of the museum was spared. The worst one affected was the lad we found close by the door."

"Lad?" McKinley asked his blood feeling like it had dropped to freezing point.

"There was a school trip here today. Most were okay. Two of them are on their way to the hospital right now and the other lad we found by the door is in the next ambulance."

"Thanks," McKinley said. "Don't let me keep you." He moved on. As he walked around to the open back door, there was Kyle, his head on a pillow and an oxygen mask over his nose and mouth. There was another paramedic, a young woman this time.

"Are you all right Sir?" she said as she saw the shock on his face.

"Th…that's my Son. How is he?" he asked climbing in.

"He's fine Sir, just taken in a bit more gas than everyone else. Apparently, this young man here," she said looking down at Kyle again, "was going after the person who committed the robbery."

"Are you taking him now?" McKinley asked.

"Yes, to GateHaven General, for observation. You're

welcome to ride along with us," she said.

"Are you sure he's all right?" he asked again.

"Yes," she said with a smile. "He's as strong as an ox. He'll be up in no time."

"I'll call his Mother and get her to meet you there," He said. "I must find out what's going on here. Would you let him know I was with him, and I'll see him as soon as I can?"

"No problem."

"Thank you for helping my boy." McKinley stepped out of the back of the ambulance. The doors closed and McKinley watched it pull out into the traffic.

After the Inspector had contacted his wife and reassured her that Kyle was okay, and which hospital she would find him, he finally made it into the main entrance. The desk in the concourse area was a flurry of activity. He spotted Sergeant Harrison and made his way through to him.

"Ah, there you are Sir," Harrison said formerly. "This is Miles Blake, Curator of the museum. Mr Blake, this is Detective Inspector McKinley."

The two men nodded and shook hands.

"Now, what can you tell us about this morning's events?" Inspector McKinley asked.

Miles shrugged. "It's pretty much been a normal day. The only thing different has been the opening of the British Battalion exhibition."

"And what about the Sapphire Spider? Has the owner been notified of its theft yet?"

"We're trying to get a hold of him as we speak," Miles replied pointing to a girl behind the desk who was arguing into a phone.

"Could you take us through to the hall?" McKinley asked gazing absently up at the skeleton suspended overhead.

"Certainly. Follow me, gentlemen," Miles said.

They could not get through the main doorway as the mangled security door that now refused to budge blocked it. Instead, they got in through a small side door, which was usually kept locked. The lab boys had already cordoned the central stand off from the rest of the room with yellow police tape. Men in white overalls were gathering up bits and pieces strewn around the floor and imprisoning them in tiny plastic bags. Some were dusting areas of the podium with a fine white powder, while others still were taking photographs of different areas of the hall.

Inspector McKinley looked from the podium to the twisted door. It must have been at least seventy feet away, quite a distance to travel if you have inhaled knockout gas.

Miles Blake spent the next five minutes going over how the robber had snatched the Spider right from under their noses and used the defence mechanisms of the museum to make the perfect getaway.

"I don't mind admitting," Miles grimaced, "He's made us look like a right bunch of idiots. He as good as walked in here, picked it up and strolled out the front door with it."

"If he got away so simply, what did that to your security door?" Harrison asked.

The two detectives and the curator went over to get a better look at it. There was one other man examining the door. He was frowning, puzzled by the extent of damage.

"What do you make of it Pinkerton?" McKinley asked as he surveyed the door himself.

Pinkerton a tall and skinny man looked at McKinley, stroking the rapier thin moustache on his top lip. "The impression given by the amount of buckling at the bottom suggests that the door had dropped, but something resisted and tried to push it back the way it came."

"Do you know the weight of the door, Mr Blake?" Inspector McKinley asked.

"Not offhand. We have all the relative paperwork regarding the security of the museum in our main office. But it's not just the weight of the door, it's also the pneumatic pressure used to drop the door once the alarm is triggered."

"If he'd have already had something in place to stop the door dropping," Pinkerton said, "it would be here now, trapped underneath the door. I don't think our thief did this. This was done by something else."

The first thing Billy was aware of was someone holding his hand. He blinked open heavy eyelids and looked up into the anxious face of his mum. Her eyes were red and puffy from crying. At the sight of Billy awake, Mrs Blake buried her face in his chest. He lay there for a minute, patting her awkwardly as he looked around. Was he in hospital?

Just then, one of the curtains swished back and a young nurse entered the cubicle.

"Ah, you're awake," she said curtly. "How are you feeling? Blurred vision? Sore throat? Anything like that?"

"No," Billy said. "Just a headache."

"That's good," The nurse said. "I'm just popping next door to check on the others. I'll be back in a few minutes."

"I was so worried," Billy's Mum said anxiously. She ran shaking fingers through Billy's hair.

"I'm fine Mum, honest," he said, but winced slightly as he moved his head too fast to avoid her combing fingers.

"Dad will be along in a short while. He's with the police now. I spoke to him on his mobile a few minutes ago before you woke up."

"I could do with something to drink," Billy said dryly.

Mrs Blake was suddenly galvanised into action. "You stay right there," she said, eager to do something for her son. She disappeared through the curtains in a blur.

Billy closed his eyes and almost at once, he found himself drifting off to sleep, but the image of what he thought he had seen before the gas had overpowered him sprang to mind.

Billy's eyes snapped open again. He sat up, ignoring the throb of his head. The nurse had said there were others here. He slipped off the bed and poked his head out the curtain. There was a small office and the nurses station at the end of the ward. Billy started walking toward it. The nurse was there talking to a Doctor in a white coat. She saw Billy and frowned.

"Billy, could wait by your bed until your Mother returns? It gets a bit hectic out here sometimes and we like to keep the corridors clear."

"Oh, right," Billy replied, "it's just that I was wondering if a friend of mine is here."

"What's his name?"

"Kyle McKinley."

The nurse scanned her bed chart. "He's in that one over there," she said pointing to a curtained off bed. "His Mother is in there at the moment, so I wouldn't go in if I were you."

Just then, Mrs Blake returned. Once back on his bed she informed Billy that his dad was on his way. An hour later Billy sat in the back of the family car heading for home. Billy was lost in his own thoughts. He didn't know why, but he had the impression that what had happened today was only the beginning.

8.

VISITING HOURS

It was over dinner that Billy found out about the security door, and that had clinched it for him. He was bursting to have a look for himself. After promises by Miles to keep an eye on their son, Mrs Blake finally agreed to let Billy go back to the museum that night. It was a little after seven o'clock when Billy and his dad pulled into a parking space outside the museum.

They were soon inside Mr Blake's office. Billy dropped into a leather bound chair as his dad removed his coat. Bookcases covered nearly all the wall spaces, all crammed to capacity. The tops were lined with glass cases displaying stuffed animals and birds, all posed with fangs or claws bared. Billy thought they must have been part of the museum's display at one time.

The False eyes glittered like jewels in the lamplight, giving the impression that they followed you around the room, which he thought were cool, in a creepy kind of way.

"Want a drink Billy?" Mr Blake asked.

"Please," Billy said.

Miles disappeared through a door in the corner of the room. He returned two minutes later with a coffee for himself and a coke for his son. He sat behind his desk.

"Billy, how well do you know the McKinley boy?"

"Why?"

"It's just that I met his father today. Do you know who he is?"

"Everyone in school knows who Kyle's Dad is," Billy said in a bored tone. "If he isn't going on about himself, then he's going on about what a brilliant police inspector his Dad is."

"Why did you hit him today?" Miles asked, eyeing Billy shrewdly.

"He...he started insulting you in front of the other kids. Isn't that enough?"

"Not really, no. I've always told you that it's all right to stick up for yourself, but don't hit first."

"You don't know what it's like Dad," Billy seethed. "He goes on at me every day, and I don't even know why."

"I don't want you to think I haven't noticed what this intimidation by McKinley has done to you. That's why I brought you along here tonight. You're going to put a stop to his bullying once and for all."

"I've tried everything Dad. I don't know what to do."

"Have you tried making friends with him?"

"That's a good one!" Billy let out a laugh that took them both by surprise. "He can't stand the sight of me."

"I know," Miles said, "and that's because you have something that he doesn't."

"And what's that?"

"A Dad that's always there for you." Miles took a big swallow from his cup.

"I don't understand?"

"Well think about it. His dad is a big noise in the GateHaven Police Force. He's out all hours of the day and night, and it's a well-known fact that the man is married to his job. I'm willing to bet my pension that Inspector McKinley sees more of his office than his family."

"I still don't see what that has to do with me," Billy sighed.

"I've been asking around," Miles went on. "I've spoken to your form teacher and headmaster about McKinley's attitude. I was very discreet about the whole thing. It turns out that McKinley's Mother is very concerned about him at the moment."

"Even so, it still doesn't give him the right."

"I agree," Miles said. "But in all the times he's confronted you, has he ever laid a hand on you?"

"No."

"I didn't think so," Miles nodded. "There's something about you McKinley likes. He's just being brash to cover it up. Discover what it is and I think the two of you will end up being friends."

Later, while Mr Blake busied himself with an important phone call, Billy was allowed to have a look around the hall. He walked over to the crumpled door, replaying the scene he saw just before he had collapsed. It was no good. He had to see McKinley. But how?

Once they were back in the car, Billy had a sudden idea.

"Dad? I've been thinking about what you said earlier, you know, about Kyle and all that."

"I'm glad to hear it." Miles smiled widely.

"In fact," Billy went on, "I'd like to see him tonight if that's all right. I thought I might have a better chance with him away from school. What do you think?"

"That might be a bit of a problem," Mr Blake said chewing his lip.

"Oh," Billy said. "Why's that?"

"Well," Mr Blake hesitated, "it seems that young Kyle is still in the hospital. Apparently there have been... complications."

Billy struggled with himself for a moment. "What's wrong with him?"

"They don't really know. I've just spoken to Mr Crane about it on the phone."

"Mr Crane?" Billy said, impressed.

"Yes," Miles said as though he spoke to multi billionaires every day. "As you know, he's on the board for the museum. He's very concerned about the theft and the condition of young McKinley."

"What's going on Dad?" Billy asked.

"According to the hospital when we enquired earlier," Miles said as he turned the car into a quieter side road, "Kyle seems to have had some sort of allergic reaction to the gas. The hospital didn't go into to too much detail since I'm not direct family."

"You don't think Kyle is putting it on do you?" Billy enquired.

Miles frowned. "Now why would he want to do a thing like that?"

"Oh come on Dad!" Billy snorted. "One of the owners of the museum is mega rich, you said so yourself. Perhaps Kyle's thinking of getting his folks to sue the museum for damages."

"You've got a devious mind on you, Bill." Miles laughed despite himself.

Billy grinned. He glanced out of the car window at the neon signs of the shops and suddenly realised that they weren't heading in the direction of home.

"Where are we going Dad?"

"Just popping into the hospital. I'm going to have a quick word with Kyle's Dad.

I'm meeting him there. I just want to know how the lad is, and how the investigation is proceeding."

"Plus Mr Crane asked you to on the phone," Billy said with a sly grin.

"It's like I just said," Miles grinned, "You've got a devious mind."

Once at the hospital, they consulted the map of the place to get their bearings. Kyle had been moved from the administration ward. He was now in ward six in a private room just off the public ward.

Miles showed Billy to the day room, where patients who could move around were allowed to go and watch television. He directed Billy to a seat and told him he would not be long.

Billy gave his dad a minute to disappear, and then he followed. He walked slowly down the corridor. As he rounded the corner, Billy saw his dad at the reception desk talking to a doctor and a man he recognised as Inspector McKinley.

Mr Blake had his back to Billy as he approached. The corridor that led into the open ward beyond had doors on either side at set intervals. These were the private side rooms, and the doors had the occupier's names written on wipeable boards. The third door along on Billy's left read "McKinley."

Just then, the door opened and a woman walked out, colliding into him. She dropped a paperback book on the floor.

"Oh!" She said, suddenly taken by surprise. "Sorry, I didn't see you there." She had short dark hair, and was not much taller than Billy himself.

"Sorry," Billy said in return, stooping to retrieve the book for her. An idea suddenly came to him. "I was looking for Kyle McKinley's room," he said as he returned the book.

"Well you've found it," she replied brightly. "I'm Kyle's Mum. What can we do for you?"

"Oh," Billy said acting surprised, "I'm one of Kyle's school friends. My Dad works for the Museum. That's him down there talking to the doctor and that other man," he said, feigning ignorance. "I just thought I'd pop in to see how Kyle is. Everyone's going to be asking about him at school tomorrow."

Mrs McKinley's face spread in a warm smile. "What a lovely thought," she said. Just then, his dad turned around and spotted him. He started heading Billy's way.

"Billy," Miles said surprised, "I thought you were waiting down the hall." Miles smiled almost apologetically to Mrs McKinley.

"Sorry," Billy said, lost for words. However, Mrs McKinley stepped in and saved the day.

"Billy here was just telling me how all the kids at school will be worrying about Kyle, so he thought he would come along so he could put everyone at ease tomorrow."

"I just thought I could see if there was anything I

could do, you know, after that talk we had earlier." Billy said his voice hopeful.

Miles smiled at his son in spite of himself. "Is it all right if Billy goes in, Mrs McKinley?"

"Certainly," she beamed. "It'll cheer him up no end to see one of his school pals."

Billy and his Dad exchanged glances. "Right then," Billy said, "I'll go in."

"No more than five minutes, Bill," his dad said.

Billy opened the door and entered. He did not know what kind of reception he was going to get, but the welcome threw him completely.

"Blake!" Kyle almost shouted in surprise as Billy closed the door behind him. His voice was full of relief and he seemed almost pleased to see him.

Billy stood there for a moment. He was puzzled, not knowing what to say next. Instead, he just nodded. Kyle was flat on his back in bed not moving a muscle.

"What brings you here?" Kyle asked, breaking the silence. "You're the last person I would have expected."

"I saw you today," Billy said finding his voice again.

He began fumbling in his pocket.

"I saw you too," Kyle said. "We were both at the museum."

"That's not what I mean and you know it," Billy replied.

"I...I don't know what you're getting at," Kyle said, his voice trying to bring on the bravado Billy was so used to hearing. McKinley looked scared.

"I saw what you did to the door at the museum," Billy said, pressing his advantage. "I saw you lift it, just before I passed out from the gas."

"The gas got you too?" Kyle asked.

"Don't change the subject. I saw you raise that door. You were crumpling it like it was made of cardboard." Billy sat in one of the chairs near the bed. "I wanted to see you anyway, to apologise for hitting you. I shouldn't have done it. And I also wanted to return this."

From his pocket, he drew out what looked like a piece of dark cloth and threw it onto the bed. Kyle slowly raised a hand and picked the cloth up where it lay. Trembling fingers slowly unfolded the creased material and he held it out before him. His eyes were wide with shock.

"You dropped it earlier in the scuffle." Billy scrutinized Kyle for a moment. McKinley's face was set like stone.

"I know it belongs to you," Billy shrugged.

"What are you going to do now?" Kyle asked in a broken voice.

Billy walked around the bed, thinking. "That depends on you. That is your mask, isn't it?"

"I don't know where to begin." Kyle's mouth was dry.

"Try starting at the beginning," Billy said eyes bright. "One way or another I'm not leaving this room until I know what's going on."

9.

MIDNIGHT VISITOR

Darius Crane paced the roof, his impatience building. Another glance at his watch told him it was a minute after twelve. He walked to the edge and peered into the darkness below.

"Don't do it Mr Crane," a dry voice said from the shadows. "You have too much to live for."

"Who the devil…" Crane spluttered, startled by the voice.

A tall man dressed in black with a long dark coat and a slouched hat stepped from a darkened corner of the roof. In his gloved hand, he carried a large black bag. He placed it down and stepped back.

"Wade?" Crane took a tentative step forward.

"Who else?"

Crane stooped to open the bag. He pulled out two packages, one larger than the other, which seemed to be made of cotton wool wadding, only thicker to the touch. Eager fingers prized the padding apart.

The two objects within made Crane catch his breath. He stretched out trembling fingers and caressed the surface of the one that interested him most. He knew it to be genuine at once, and lifted it as if it was a newborn baby.

"You've done well Mr Wade." Crane looked down at the second object to come from the bag. "Why on earth did you take that in the first place?"

"It drew attention away from what I was really after at the museum today." Wade said.

"You certainly caused a commotion all right," Crane replied, and picked up the Sapphire Spider. The jewels on the legs caught the light and glittered as if alive.

"No one is able to point the finger of suspicion at you. That is why I took it in such a manner."

"Do you really imagine that the public would think that a man of my standing would rob his own museum?"

"Who knows?" Wade said, "But either way, you'll never be suspected now."

Crane placed the two items back in the bag and zipped it shut. "I can even turn this around; make it look like I retrieved the Spider unaided."

"I was thinking along the same tracks too," Wade said.

"Were you indeed? I suppose it's a way of repaying for the damage to that rather expensive security door."

"That wasn't me," Wade replied. "My escape route had already been planned out. Someone was chasing after me. As I was leaving, someone on the other side of the door was trying to lift it out of the way. The door jammed because it was twisted out of shape. He was wearing a school uniform," he added quietly.

Crane shook his head. "Say that again Mr Wade, I don't think I heard you properly."

"Oh, you heard me all right. There was a school trip to the museum today. Several of the children were in the hall when I took the Spider."

Crane scratched his chin thoughtfully. "What is your current employment situation like Mr Wade?"

Billy was in a bad frame of mind the following morning at school. Just when it looked as if McKinley was going to reveal all, Billy's dad returned saying that it was time to leave.

According to Mr Miller at class registration, Kyle was still in for observation. Some of the girls in the class were actually crying. Jen on the other hand sat silently beside him. She had questioned him when he first entered the class, but he had managed to reassure her he was fine. Jen had then reached under the desk and squeezed his hand, refusing to let go. He grinned side long at her, his face flushing. Someone called his name and he turned to see Mr Miller looking at him.

"Billy, would you stay behind after registration; there's something I need to discuss with you."

"Uhh, sure," Billy answered slowly, wondering what he had done wrong now. As the rest of the class filed out to go off to their first lessons of the day, Jenny paused at the door, waiting for him. Mr Miller shooed her away with a wave of his hand.

"How are you this morning?" Mr Miller asked.

"I'm fine," Billy said flashing a smile to back up his statement.

"Are you sure you're up to a full day here? Maybe after the police have interviewed you, you might think about going home and resting up for a while."

Billy started. "The police want to interview me?"

"They're seeing everyone that was on the trip yesterday. Just make your way to the head's office; the police are interviewing there. You're the first. It shouldn't take too long,"

"Why me first?" Billy asked his voice shrill with panic.

Billy soon found himself outside the office. A knot of worry was tying itself sharply in his stomach. He took a moment to compose himself then knocked lightly on the door.

A voice bid him enter. Instead of the headmaster, Billy found himself looking at Inspector McKinley.

"Morning Billy," he said with a broad smile, "Take a seat would you? We need to clarify a few things in order to speed up our investigation, so we're asking everyone who was present in the museum yesterday to help us with our inquiries."

It took Billy several minutes to tell his side of events as he remembered them. All the while he talked, McKinley returned his gaze, hardly seeming to blink.

"-and that was when the room filled with gas," Billy said finally. "I don't really remember much after that."

"Did you happen to see in which direction the burglar ran to make his escape?"

"Sure," Billy said nodding. "He made straight for the door. He was moving fast for an old bloke though. Do you reckon he had on some sort of disguise, Inspector?"

"That was our assumption, yes," McKinley replied. "The door he ran through met with some kind of accident. Did you happen to see what caused the door to become bent like that?"

Billy shook his head. "No Sir. I heard it though. It's the last thing I can remember before blacking out."

"Now think hard Billy, are you sure you didn't see anything?" McKinley asked, leaning forward.

Billy shrugged. "It's difficult to say Sir. The room was full of gas. I thought I saw someone but I can't swear to it."

"Who do you think it could have been?" McKinley asked.

"I think it was the old man," he said finally, after pretending to give the matter some considerable thought.

"Are you sure?"

" All I know is that I saw Kyle trying to give chase, but the gas had already taken effect. He hit the deck like a sack of potatoes before he made it to the door. That must have been when I passed out too."

Billy could see something like relief flicker momentarily across the inspector's face. The next ten minutes were spent going over things again to make sure they had all the facts.

"Inspector, I think I am going to go home now," Billy said when they had finished. "This headache of mine is getting worse. Would it be all right if I called in on Kyle to see how he's doing?"

"I don't see why not," Inspector McKinley said. "He's coming home tonight anyway and should be back at school in a day or two. Would you like a lift to the hospital?"

After telling the secretary in the school office that he was going home, Billy was driven to the hospital by police car. Soon he was standing outside the door to Kyle's room. Billy took a deep breath and entered. Kyle sat on the edge of his bed. Billy stepped into the room and closed the door behind him.

"I thought you'd be back," Kyle said. Billy was surprised to see that he had the mask in his hands.

"I've been telling your dad what I saw at the museum yesterday, or at least what I thought I saw," Billy replied quietly.

"You want the truth?" Kyle asked, meeting Billy's gaze and holding it.

"Take your time," Billy said quietly. "I've got all day."

10.

TRUTH BE TOLD

The room was silent as the two boys looked at each other. Finally, Kyle said, "Could you pass me that empty vase on the window sill?"

Billy handed it over. It was metallic, its sides rising up to a thin neck. Closing his hand around the vase, Kyle applied pressure and crushed it as if it was the silver foil off a chocolate bar.

Billy gaped. "How did you do that?"

"I don't know." Kyle flexed his fingers as though his hand didn't belong to him. "I don't know what's happening to me."

Billy stood up. "Okay. So tell me what the mask is

all about."

"I'm the Grey-Ghost," Kyle grimaced.

"Who?" Billy said, his mouth turning up at the edges as he tried to suppress a grin.

"You see," Kyle scowled. "I knew you'd laugh. And I thought that you of all people would understand."

"Understand what?"

"I want to fight crime." Kyle said with no hint of humour. "I want to help."

"You mean like a super hero?"

"I know it sounds mad. Don't you think I know how it sounds?"

"But you hate super heroes," Billy replied. "That's why you pick on me."

"No," Kyle said firmly. "I pick on you because I love comics too, only my dad won't let me read them. He says they're childish."

Billy could feel his own temper suddenly rising. "And that gave you the excuse to pick on me?"

"What can I say?" Kyle shook his head sadly. "I'm sorry. I know that doesn't make up for what I've done to you. I intended to give the idea to the other kids at school that I thought comics were childish. It's the secret identity thing. Nearly always in comics, the hero's everyday identity is the wimp who is being pushed around by the bullies.

"If I was going to do this seriously, I needed to come up with a way where people would never suspect that Grey-Ghost was me. So I thought the spotlight would be off me. Things just got a little out of hand, that's all," Kyle added in a small voice.

"Oh, you mean like, picking on me every single minute of every school day? Well that's not good enough." Billy's voice was strangled with anger. A torrent of abuse spilled out of him like a flooded river bursting its banks. Billy held nothing back as he told Kyle how miserable he had made his school life.

Kyle sat there and took it. He knew he deserved it, and everything Billy was bellowing at him was true. He had started out with the noblest of intentions, but it had run away with itself, just like a snowball rolling downhill.

"You know my secret," Kyle said when Billy had finally exhausted himself. "Are you going to tell anyone?"

"I haven't made my mind up," Billy seethed.

"I wouldn't blame you if you did, but that's the least of my worries right now."

"Why?"

Kyle looked up at him. "Because I'm scared. I don't know how strong I am. My movements feel different, like being in a body that I'm not used to. What if I can't control this strength? What if I end up hurting, or even killing someone?" Kyle's eyes had a sudden hollow look about them.

"Calm down Kyle," Billy said in a quiet voice, "Panicking won't get you anywhere will it?" Most of the anger that Billy felt had subsided. It was replaced by a growing curiosity.

"When were you first aware of your strength?" Billy pursed his lips as he started to pace the room.

"The door at the museum," Kyle replied, his eyes following Billy to the far end of the room and back again.

"What made you think you could stop such a heavy door from shutting?"

"I just knew I could stop it, I don't know how. All I could think of was that I had to stop the thief. He couldn't just get away like that."

"Why?" Billy asked bluntly, as he stopped his pacing. "Why did you have to stop him?"

"Because it was the right thing to do."

"Is that what you always try to do...the right thing?"

"Yes, I suppose so," Kyle replied.

"Was picking on me at school the right thing to do?" Billy suddenly asked eyes bright with anger again.

"No," Kyle said with regret. "Picking on you was wrong. I should have found another way. It was just that..." his voice trailed off. A shocking realisation occurred to him. Before Kyle could help himself, the words spilled out.

"I'm jealous of you."

"What?" Billy said, wide eyed with disbelief.

All the while the two boys had been going at it; the television in the corner of the room had been on with the sound off. Billy happened to glance at it and saw something that caught his eye.

"Kyle, turn the telly up," he said quickly. Kyle did as he was asked, pressing the mute button on the remote.

There before them on the TV screen stood none other than Darius Crane with the Sapphire Spider in his hands. He was surrounded by reporters. The TV screen suddenly cut to the news studio, where a reporter sat behind a desk was speaking to the camera.

"For those of you who have just joined us, the fabled Sapphire Spider has been recovered by philanthropist Darius Crane. The Spider was taken on Tuesday morning in a daring heist at the GateHaven Natural History Museum.

"Mr Crane says the Spider came to him by way of an anonymous tip late last night. It would appear that the priceless arachnid was too hot to handle.

"He went on to say that he felt personally responsible for the theft, since the Spider was on show in his museum. Mr Crane will spend the rest of the day at GateHaven, where apart from visiting his museum, he will stop by the hospital, where several members of the public were taken after the heist yesterday..."

"Surely he can't mean here?" Billy said.

Kyle looked from the TV and was about to answer, when there was a sudden

commotion in the corridor outside. The door opened wide and a whole gaggle of people walked in on them.

"What's going on?" Kyle asked, as the room was suddenly full to bursting with TV camera crew, reporter, and soundmen. In the middle of it, stood Darius Crane.

By the open door Billy could make out two enormous men dressed in dark suits and sunglasses, bodyguards no doubt for Mr Crane. Billy's eyes swivelled back to the man standing right at Kyle's bedside.

Crane was over six feet in height, about fifty years old Billy reckoned, and was completely bald. He wore a moustache and goatee beard that was silver in colour. Far from making Mr Crane look old, what with the dark tan and the cold blue eyes, he looked very fit and seemed to radiate power, as if he demanded your attention when in the room. He was wearing a dark green two-piece suit that looked as if it cost more money than Billy's dad earned in six months

The man was all smiles.

"And here's the lad himself," Crane said as he partially turned to address the news camera. "The hero of the day."

Hero?" Kyle said in a worried voice. He scanned the room for Billy, who was standing forgotten over by the window.

"Now don't be modest, Kyle," Crane said with a wide grin. "We all know what you did yesterday at the museum. It was a brave thing, but you could have been hurt, or worse. I only hope that you have learned something from this, and realised that the police should handle this sort of thing.

"I'd just like to say thank you to the staff here at the hospital for taking such great care of the school kids, and that The Crane Corporation will be making a sizeable donation towards new medical equipment as our way of showing our gratitude."

There was a smattering of applause, from outside the room this time as nurses and patients alike had gathered to listen to Crane's impassioned speech.

He held up his hands once more. "I think it's about time I shut up," he said. Crane beamed and held out a hand. Kyle hesitated. As Crane's hand closed over Kyle's, both man and boy jumped as skin touched skin, almost as if an electric charge had passed between them.

They both broke contact reflexively, Crane staring at his palm and then at Kyle.

"I don't know about medical equipment," Crane said shaking his hand and grinning, "I think we'll be supplying the hospital with new sheets for the beds. These man-made fabrics really pack a wallop with all the static electricity they build up, don't they Kyle?"

Kyle nodded and smiled weakly as the rest of the room burst into laughter. At that moment, a doctor made his presence known.

"I think it's time that we all leave Kyle to some much earned peace and quiet. He'll be leaving our care later today so I want him to rest as much as he can."

"You heard the man everybody," Crane chirped in. "We've outstayed our welcome. It was a real pleasure meeting you Kyle. Perhaps when you're back on your feet, you and your family would like to join my wife and I for dinner."

The doctor and nurses began herding the reporters out the door. Two minutes later the boys found themselves on their own again, after several nurses had been in to straighten the room.

"What was that all about?" Kyle said bewildered.

"I don't know," Billy replied.

Kyle was looking at the hand that Crane had just shaken.

Billy frowned. "What is it?"

"I don't know," Kyle said almost distractedly. "When he touched me, I felt a sudden...weakness for a moment. It stopped as soon as he let go."

"So you didn't get a jolt off the sheets?"

"I don't know what it was, but it wasn't anything like that."

Billy glanced at his watch. "I'm going to be late for tea," he said as he backed slowly toward the door. "I guess I'll be seeing you at school tomorrow then."

"If mum let's me go," Kyle said with a shrug. "I still

don't know what to make of all this."

"Just take it slowly," Billy replied as he opened the door.

"Hold on, you can't just leave like that," Kyle said almost in a panic. "Have you decided if you're going to help me or not?"

"I really don't know. There's too much going on. I'm going to have to sleep on it."

And with that, the door closed behind Billy, leaving Kyle alone and wondering where he went from there.

11.

TRIAL & ERROR

When it was time for Kyle to leave hospital that evening, the press were camped outside. Inspector McKinley whisked his son away in a squad car before the journalists could get too close. Soon, Kyle laid stretched out on the sofa at home, eyes closed and already breathing deeply.

"Didn't take him long to drop off," his mum said as she laid a hand on his forehead. "He should be in bed."

"He's already resting," Bob McKinley replied. "It won't do him any harm to stay there a while." He looked around the room. "Where's Cassandra?"

"She's already in bed. Packed her off upstairs about half an hour ago."

The Inspector's mobile phone rang. He fished it out of his pocket. This was his works phone so he headed toward the kitchen door for some privacy.

Sue McKinley had a questioning look on her face when he returned. "What is it, Bob?"

"I've got to go to the station. Something to do with the museum and the recovered jewels. I shouldn't be more than an hour."

"But what about Kyle?"

"Let him sleep. I'll be back before he wakes up."

"Can't someone cover for you?" Mrs McKinley asked hopefully.

"No," he said sighing. "The bigwigs upstairs have asked for me personally."

"Your son needs you," Sue said pointing with emphasis at Kyle asleep on the sofa. "What do I tell him if he wakes up and asks for you?"

"Don't do this to me, Sue," the Inspector said with a pained look on his face. "We're stretched for manpower as it is. Look, we'll talk about his when I get back." He stooped slightly and kissed his wife. Moments later the door was closing behind him.

He had fallen asleep the moment his head touched the cushion. After a while, he was aware of someone watching him. Kyle opened his eyes, only to find his sister staring at him.

"What's up?" he said weakly.

"Are you feeling better now?" Cassie asked as she smiled back.

"Oh, yeah, just a little tired that's all."

"Are you going to school tomorrow?" she checked him from head to foot for any signs of injuries, bandages or plasters of any kind.

"No, mum won't let me."

"Why not, I can't see anything wrong with you." Cassie whined. "I've got a cold and mum makes me go to school. It's not fair! Mum wouldn't let me go to the hospital to visit you in case I picked up more germs." Her face suddenly brightened and she nudged her big brother in the side with a pointed elbow.

"You were on the telly tonight. Was it exciting? Are

you going to be an actor now?" she asked her brown eyes as wide as saucers.

For the first time in two days, Kyle grinned. He told Cassie all that had happened at the museum, the robbery, the gas attack, and his stay in hospital.

"Anyway," he said finally, "time you were back in bed. You'll cop it if mum finds you down here."

"Will you take me?" Cassie held her hand out for Kyle to take it.

He looked at her small hand and bit his lip nervously. "Can't you go on your own?"

"No, I want you to take me." And with that, she grabbed Kyle's hand and tried to yank him to his feet.

Kyle flinched at her touch and was suddenly aware of how much bigger his hand was than hers. He could break every bone without even trying. Slowly, Kyle let his fingers close as gently as possible. With Cassie leading the way, they climbed the stairs to the upper landing. When they made it to her room, Cassie slipped out of his grip and sprang for her bed, snuggling down into the quilt.

"I'll see you tomorrow then," Kyle said, and was halfway out the door when Cassie called him back.

"Kyle?"

"Yes?"

"Why are you walking so slowly?"

"Just tired I guess," Kyle replied, which wasn't far from the truth. "I'll be fine after a good night's sleep."

"Could you leave the landing light on for me?"

"Sure." He pulled her bedroom door too so that just enough light filtered through.

Sometime later, he sat watching the evening news. His mum was in the bath and dad hadn't returned from the station. Nothing new there, Kyle thought glumly. His dad practically lived there nowadays. It was really starting to get to Mum. He'd heard his parents arguing about it before, but just lately it seemed to be getting worse. It was as if Dad didn't have time for them anymore.

Later, as he went to bed he thought of Cassie's hand in his again, and shuddered. Something was going to have to be done about his strength and the sooner the better!

Dad had returned from work late and had spent the rest of the evening in the kitchen discussing things with Mum. Eventually his parents went to bed. Now the house was asleep.

Kyle quietly got out of bed, already dressed in the dark suit. He hastily made a rough body shape beneath the quilt with his pillows. If his folks were to look in on him while he was gone, it would look like he was fast asleep.

Grey-Ghost quietly opened the window as wide as possible. Climbing out onto the window ledge, he looked at the same tree he had tried to leap to just three nights ago. There was no doubt in his mind that he could reach it now. But what if he used too much strength?

Ghost looked down at the patio below. Perhaps that was the best way to go. Could he drop that far without hurting himself? There was only one way to find out. He landed noiselessly, curling into a low crouch. He hadn't felt so much as a twinge of pain, a twisted ankle or anything.

He ran at a low crouch to the top end of the garden,

easily picking his way through the dark, and it occurred to him as he ran that his eyes must be stronger as well. He could now see far better in the dark than ever. Noiselessly he reached the back fence that blocked the garden off from the street beyond.

The fencing was six feet in height, topped off with decorative lattice. His cable strong fingers got a firm hold and he tensed himself again ready to vault over to the path on the other side. He jumped, but so strong was his leap that he lost his grip and sailed up into the air, more than clearing it by twice its height.

Ghost came down to earth on the other side, his arms and legs wind milling wildly out of control. He landed more in a heap this time.

He picked himself up and started to jog down the deserted street, careful to keep to the shadows. The jog became a run as he gradually picked up the pace and was soon sprinting flat out. He had always been a good runner, and had represented his school at several distances.

Now, Ghost knew he was beyond good. He knew

he was beyond Olympic level speeds as he literally flew down the road, his arms and legs a blur of motion and power. Before he knew it, he was approaching the main road into town. It would be busier than the estate he was currently running through. The only safe place he could go to test himself was the Rec, an adventure playground for kids that lay on the meadow the other side of the main road.

Ghost put in an extra kick and within moments was running across open grassland. He ran slower this time, trying to gauge his strength, getting used to the feeling of his body as he pounded through the dewy grass. He looked around, marvelling at how easily he could see in the dark.

A minute later, he was entering the Rec. It was a mass of steel climbing frames, seesaws, slides, swings and roundabouts. All the kids from the local area came here to play, or meet after school.

Now though, it was just Ghost and a fox or two. He spent ten minutes doing chin-ups on the bars, losing count. He did sit-ups, testing even his stomach muscles.

He used to be able to do fifty before the pain would become too much to continue. Now it was over three hundred and he wasn't getting so much as a twinge. He used the open grassland to somersault about without having to worry about crashing into anything.

Ghost put all his gymnastic training to good use as he leaped and flipped in a variety of combinations as he imagined himself avoiding gunfire from some criminal he had tracked down to their hideout. He did standing jumps to see how far forward he could leap. Not having a tape measure with him, he couldn't be sure, but he reckoned he could clear over forty feet. If he took a running jump it was twice the distance at least.

The Grey-Ghost performed a standing high jump, and after an hour's practise, he reckoned he could easily jump up onto the roof of a two-floored house. He took time leaping for the climbing bars, learning to judge how much strength to use. Once or twice he had crashed into the bars, having overdone it, and once missing the bars altogether, sailing over them as he had done the fence back home.

Ghost eventually looked at the glowing face of his watch hidden beneath his glove. It was now well after three in the morning. He wasn't tired in the least, but he didn't think it wise to push his luck. He retraced his steps back through the meadow, running at a steady rate, which happened to be faster than anyone else could possibly run at a sprint, and was back at the garden fence in a matter of minutes.

Ghost paused to check it was clear. He sprang over the fence with much more control than before. He sneaked through the garden to the patio and found himself looking up at his bedroom windowsill. He got it on the second try, hauling himself effortlessly into his room. Within minutes, he was out of costume and beneath the quilt. Kyle drifted off into a dreamless sleep, a small smile twitching the corners of his mouth.

12.

THE NOTE

Thursday for Kyle was spent at home. Everyone else was out, but he wasn't alone for long. There was a knock at the front door. To his surprise, the person standing there was Billy Blake.

Kyle gaped for a moment. "What-what are you doing here?" he stammered.

"I've finished school early again today. Told them I still have a bit of a headache. Once I knew you were absent, I wanted find out what was going on. Can I come in?"

"Uhh... sure." Kyle ushered Billy through to the living room and sat in the chair opposite.

There was a strained silence between the two boys

as they stared at everything else in the room except each other. Kyle was the first to speak up.

"You coming here, does this mean you're going to help me?"

"I...I guess it does," Billy looked at Kyle with a shocked expression.

Kyle grinned, but it soon withered away to be replaced by a sudden look of shame.

"Look, I can't apologise enough for the way I've been. There's no excuse for what I've done, but I want you to know it stops right here, and...and I'll do everything I can to make up for it."

Billy just nodded. "That's now behind us. If we're going to solve the mystery of your powers, we'll only do it acting as a team. Agreed?"

"Agreed," Kyle said and nodded. "But I need to explain the way I've been acting toward-"

"It's okay," Billy said interrupting him. "There'll be time for that later. Do you have a pen and paper?" he asked clearing away a space on the coffee table between them.

The two boys sat for the next two hours going over the events of Tuesday. Kyle retold his fainting spell. He admitted tripping and knocking himself out had been a lie, and had actually been in the Viking exhibition when it happened.

Finally, Billy glanced at his watch. "Oops, time for me to go. Will you be at school tomorrow?" he asked his face suddenly mask-like.

"I think mum wants me to take the day off, since it's Friday and I'll have the weekend to recover ready for next week."

"I suppose in order to maintain that everything is normal, I'm going to become your favourite target again," said Billy resigned to the fact.

"No," Kyle said, "that won't be happening."

"Sure," said Billy with a snort, "once you get back among your crowd, they'll expect nothing less."

"Well, they're going to be disappointed, aren't they?" said Kyle, his voice firm.

"We'll see." Billy rose from his seat. He smiled weakly and made his way to the door, Kyle following him.

As Kyle opened the door, he said, "I give you my word, things will be different."

Billy just shrugged. "I might see you tomorrow, then."

Kyle shrugged. "I hope so."

Billy was making his way home when he suddenly changed direction, and headed for the museum. Once there, he made straight for the Viking hall. Billy weaved his way around the room looking at the artefacts; he had to admit to himself that he didn't have the first clue what he was looking for.

Nevertheless, he continued his search, glancing in all the cabinets for the slightest clue to the mystery he had set himself to solve. After another ten minutes, Billy had convinced himself that he was wasting his time.

Then something caught his eye.

It was with a feeling of dread that Billy awoke on Friday morning. Moreover, by the time he had taken his seat for morning registration, he was feeling sick to his stomach.

"What's wrong?" Jen asked in a quiet voice. "You've been quiet all the way to school. You're not in any trouble are you?"

Billy shook his head. "Just got something on my mind, that's all." Just then, the colour drained from his face as Kyle entered the classroom.

Most of the class made a dash toward him. Hands clapped McKinley on the back, as he became the hero of the hour once again. Kyle made his way toward the back of the class, and as he passed Billy and Jen's desk, Kyle did not even look at him.

Friday morning was a school assembly morning. The main hall was easily the largest room in the school, its ceiling rising twenty feet above them, the walls panelled in dark wood, and the windows set high. At the far end of the hall was the raised stage, where the school plays and concerts were performed.

When all the years had filed in, Mr English the headmaster approached the front of the stage looking out over the heads of the children.

"Good morning school," he began brightly, "before I

read out any notices, we'll all sing 'Morning Has Broken' together. He pointed to a screen behind him where the words to the song were shining from a word projector for the students to read. The piano struck up and the whole school launched into an awful rendition. Mr English seemed unaware of the cacophony as he belted out the tune with gusto.

As the song finished and the school fell silent, Mr English read out some notices about school activities that were coming up over the next week.

"And lastly," Mr English said after he had finished, "it gives me great pleasure to welcome Kyle McKinley back to our number. I'm pleased to say that he has made a full recovery, and we all look forward to seeing him scoring more goals for the school team in the coming season ahead. But first, if he would care to join me…"

The crowd parted to allow Kyle to make his way through to the stage. Mr English had Kyle go over the events of the robbery for the rest of the school to hear. Kyle retold the tale almost parrot fashion, with no hint of embarrassment whatsoever.

"...And finally I'd just like to thank Billy Blake for helping out at the museum on Tuesday. I wouldn't have had the bottle to go after the thief if I'd been on my own." Kyle located Billy's stunned face in the crowd and pointed.

The silence was palpable as everyone swivelled to look at Billy's ever-reddening face.

"This is certainly news to me," Mr English said.

"Well, Billy's being modest I guess," Kyle grinned.

"Billy, could you approach the front please," The headmaster prompted.

Billy, his face glowing like the setting sun approached the podium. He stared back out over the rest of the kids, finding Jen's face among the rest of his year. She was beaming at him.

"Well you certainly are a dark horse, Billy," said Mr English in an astonished tone. "Why keep this to yourself?"

"I...I didn't want to make a fuss," Billy stammered.

"Well fuss or not, we're all glad that you weren't hurt in any way. And the school is very proud of the pair of you." Mr English clapped, the whole school following his lead.

"I told you I'd change things," Kyle said as he leaned in close to Billy so only he could hear.

"Now that everybody knows what went on during the robbery," Mr English said as the applause subsided, "I want Kyle and Billy to be allowed to get on with their schoolwork with no further interruptions. As far as I'm concerned the matter is closed and we teachers want the school to get back to normal."

By the time Billy had made it back to class to pick up his bag, he reckoned half the school had congratulated him as they passed him in the hall. Jen was jabbering in his ear about how she couldn't believe it.

"It looks like all your troubles are over," she beamed as she picked her bag off her desk ready to go off to the first lesson. "Meet you in the canteen for lunch; you can tell me all about it."

Billy grinned. "You heard Mr English," he said, "He wants the matter dropped."

"Yeah, but this is me," Jen said. She reached across the

desk, gave Billy's hand a quick squeeze, and hurried off.

He stared after. He was becoming more and more confused about Jen. He knew she liked him, but the way she was acting lately, did this mean she wanted to be his Girl-

The thought was cut short as Kyle came through the door, his face ashen. He made straight for Billy with a look of sheer panic on his face. Not knowing how to react to Kyle at school, Billy reflexively took a step back.

"Look what I found in my locker," Kyle said in a harsh whisper, and he handed Billy a crumpled note.

Startled, Billy held it up and read it.

> *I* KNOW YOUR SECRET.
> MEET ME TONIGHT AT
> MIDNIGHT
> ON THE ROOF OF THE
> MONOLITH HOTEL.
> DO NOT DISAPOINT ME!

"This was in your locker?"

Kyle nodded. "It wasn't even broken into. They knew the combination number." Kyle frowned. "How could they possibly know? What am I going to do?"

"Nothing. Just go about things as normal. We don't have any lessons together today. It's just as well judging by the way your cronies were looking at me."

"Don't worry about them," Kyle said almost distractedly. "They won't lay a finger on you."

"Even so, let's just take it slow with this newfound friendship of ours, okay?"

Kyle thought about it, and then said, "Understood."

"I'll come round to your place tonight after school. I'll walk home with Jen as normal, then double back."

"You're taking this a lot easier than me," Kyle said. "Why?"

"I would have thought that was obvious," Billy said with a shrug. "Whoever it is, wants you, not me. Don't worry for the moment," he said in a quick tone, "but you're going have to meet this person, whoever it is. But this time, Grey-Ghost won't be alone."

"What do you mean?" Kyle asked.

"I'm coming with you." Billy said. Before Kyle could protest, Billy had turned the corner and was gone.

13.

HEAVY BURDEN

Both boys had gone to bed at their respective houses a little after ten o'clock. At eleven thirty, the two of them made their move. They met at the Rec. Billy was on his mountain bike, while Grey-Ghost was on foot. As it was, Billy could hardly keep up.

Now they were crouched on a rooftop directly across from the Monolith. The night wind whipped at Ghost's mask as he looked out over the street toward the old Hotel. It had been closed for years. The only things to inhabit it were the rats.

"How are you going to get over there?" Billy asked through chattering teeth. The October wind at that height was cutting through his clothes.

"I'm gonna jump across,"

"But we're fifteen floors up," Billy gaped, "suppose you fall? You'll be dead and I'll be stuck up here!"

"I won't fall, Billy," Grey-Ghost said. "I know I can jump the gap between these two buildings. What time is it?"

Billy pressed a button that illuminated the face of his watch. "Eleven fifty eight. Are you ready?"

"No, but I'd better get going. Now remember," Ghost replied, "whatever happens, stay right here."

Billy shrugged. "I don't think I can get off this roof without your help."

Ghost gave Billy the thumbs up, then turned and approached the edge of the roof. There was a sheer drop beneath him, and he knew that however strong he had become, there was no way he could survive the fall.

Ghost backed up to give him room for a running jump. He took several long strides and kicked off from the gravel roof, sailing across the yawning chasm. He landed in a crouch on the Monolith rooftop just as planned.

"You should think about competing in the next Olympics," A voice announced from one of the darkened corners of the roof.

"Who's that?" Grey-Ghost spun around. No one was there.

"You first," the voice urged. "I know you're Kyle McKinley, but what's with the costume?"

"I'm the Grey-Ghost."

"That's a cool name. Something happened to you at the museum the other day, didn't it?"

"Yes. How do you know?"

"Because it was me you were chasing after."

"You were the old man at the museum?' Ghost squinted at the darkest corner.

"That's right," the voice replied.

"What do you want?' Ghost asked, eyes raking every inch of the roof and finding nothing.

"I want to help."

"I don't need any help," Ghost retorted.

"Yes you do. You just don't know it yet. There's someone after you. This someone is used to getting what he wants. And this someone doesn't let anything get in his way."

"Who is he?"

"Darius Crane. Perhaps you've heard of him?"

"You must be joking." Ghost started edging toward the far end of the roof. "Why would Crane be after me?"

"I'm afraid I don't have the answer to that one. He knows what happened at the museum, which was the reason why he came to visit you at the hospital."

"You know about that?" Ghost asked. He thought he saw movement on the other roof. Was it Billy shifting around?

"It was on television for everyone to see. Was I mistaken, or was there something going on between the two of you?"

"I'm saying nothing until you show yourself," Ghost said.

"Look, I mean you no harm. Ask yourself a question: what's to stop me putting a bullet through your head right now? It's obvious you're new to the game. I mean to say, you brought your friend along with you. What was he going to do, cheer you on?"

And Grey-Ghost knew where the mystery voice was hiding. He sprinted for the far end of the roof, kicking gravel as he returned the way he had come. He threw himself headlong across the gap separating him from Billy.

As he landed, Billy stood in the shadow of a large chimneystack. Ghost could see fear written all over his new friend's face. The reason for his fear stood behind him with a gloved hand resting lightly on his shoulder.

He was tall, over six feet in height, dressed head to toe in black. He wore a long, dark coat that hung down to his booted feet. No features were visible, as he too wore a mask with opaque lenses.

"Okay," Ghost said with a shaky voice, "you've made your point, now let my friend go."

Much to his surprise, the masked man released his grip on Billy's shoulder, and after a moment's hesitation, Billy turned and backed slowly away.

"You see," said the man in black, "I mean neither of you any harm." He didn't move, but held his hands out, palms upward. "Now will you listen to me?"

Ghost launched himself at the man in black. At the last instant, his target sprang sideways which took him away from Grey-Ghost's clutches.

Ghost went sprawling, headlong into the chimneystack. Blinking away the stars, he looked around quickly and found the man perched on top of the chimney, like a gargoyle, unmoving.

"What do you think you're doing?" the man in black said in a puzzled tone. "I've already told you that I don't want to hurt you. There is nothing to be gained by fighting. Besides," he added, almost bored, "you don't stand a chance."

"Is that a fact?" Ghost said as he renewed his attack. By the time he made it to the chimney top, his target was no longer there. A moment later, he located him again, standing behind Billy.

"Stop this, Kyle," he said sounding irritated.

"You stole the Spider. In my book that makes you one of the bad guys,"

"I had my reasons for what I did," the man in black

said. "Give me a chance and I'll explain everything."

Ghost was already moving. Billy had edged away enough to leave an open target. He took off like a missile. So fast was his attack that the two of them went down in a flurry of arms and legs.

Seconds later, the masked man came to his feet first, cart wheeling away from Grey-Ghost, who was already climbing swiftly to his feet.

"I'll put it down to the fact that you're itching to test your new powers, that's why you want to fight me," the man in black said, almost laughing. "Okay, let's get it over with shall we?"

Ghost covered the gap between them in the blink of an eye, and almost made contact again, but the man in black dropped to the cold roof, and Ghost sailed clear over him.

"Who are you?" Ghost asked as he circled around, trying to get closer.

"You can call me Wade," the man in black said as he did the unexpected, and took the fight to Kyle.

Wade leapt forward, grasping the Ghost by the

shoulders, while at the same time tucking a leg around his opponent's and pushing forward. Ghost went sprawling on his behind.

"That was a basic throw and you fell for it, literally," Wade said with a laugh as he sprang away again.

"You deserve to be in prison," Ghost said through gritted teeth, his anger barely held in check.

"Why, because I steal things from people who are so rich that they wouldn't even miss the objects I've 'borrowed'?"

"Stealing is stealing," Ghost said trying to get within range of Wade.

"You don't know the first thing about me," Wade barked, "so don't go all noble on me and tell me what's right or wrong. This is the real world you're in now. The good guys don't always wear the white hats."

Ghost sprang and swung what he thought was a well-aimed punch at Wade's head, but his fist connected with the wall. Fragments of brick flew everywhere.

"Who's the good guy now?" Wade asked from somewhere over the Ghost's shoulder. "If your punch had made contact with my head, do you think I could have survived it? Plus, you've just caused criminal damage to someone's wall."

"I...I didn't think..." Ghost began, his voice shaking.

"And that's your problem," Wade said as he hopped down from his perch. "Listen," he began in a quiet voice, but whatever he was going to say next died on his lips as a crashing sound, and the crunching of metal split the quiet of the night.

Ghost, Wade, and Billy looked at each other, and then all three of them were racing for the edge of the roof.

"Oh my god," Ghost heard Wade hiss through clenched teeth. He was looking through a very compact, but sophisticated set of binoculars he had pulled out from the folds of his coat.

"There's been a collision. A car and a truck. It looks like someone's pinned underneath. You've got to get down there, quick!"

It took a moment for the last statement to sink in. "Me?" Ghost said, shocked. "Why me?"

"Because you're the only one who has the slightest

chance of saving that person." Wade pulled the goggles away from his eyes and looked into Kyle's masked face. "Are you ready?"

"What-" Ghost stammered.

Wade didn't wait for an answer as he hopped up onto the roofs ledge. He felt inside one of the pockets and pulled out what looked like a small gun with a tiny spear sticking out of the end. Wade pulled the trigger, and the spear shot into the concrete ledge, embedding itself firmly. Attached was a very slender piece of cable. When Wade had exhausted the gun, he put it away and pulled out something else, which he wrapped around the cable.

"We're fifteen floors up," Wade said very businesslike as more screams reached their ears. "The cable is good enough for ten. Do you think you can drop the last five?"

"Possibly," Ghost said, looking at Billy, who looked scared.

"Take the end of this," Wade said and offered the item he'd wrapped around the cable.

"What is it?" Ghost asked his mouth very dry. It

looked like a tube with indents in it for finger grips. It was springy, and as he closed his fist around it, so it gripped the cable running through its length.

"Just take it and hold on tight. It'll let you descend the cable without it slicing your fingers off. Squeeze it harder to slow your descent."

"This won't hold my weight," Grey-Ghost said with a shaking voice.

"Yes it will. Listen to me. Someone is under that lorry. If you don't get down there right now, they're going to die." Wade glanced at Ghost's costume. "You've chosen to be a hero haven't you?"

"Yes," Grey-Ghost replied.

"Be that hero now. Save those people. We'll watch until you've gotten them to safety, then we'll meet you on the roof of the Metro Cinema. Now go! ***GO!***"

Ghost took a moment to glance below, then without thinking, he stepped off the safety of his perch into the night air. He went down like a rocket, the cord slipping through his hand as if it was alive. The street rushed up to meet him quicker than he thought possible. What was it he had to do to slow himself down? Then he remembered and squeezed the grip around the cord His speed slowed almost immediately, and he squeezed even harder as he saw the end of the cord shooting up to meet him.

Ghost came to a halt just before the cord shot through his grip completely. He hung there for a moment, still five floors above the street. He wasn't one hundred percent sure if he could do the rest of the way without breaking something, so he cast about for something to jump down onto, and saw the perfect thing.

Bracing his legs against the wall, he kicked off, letting go of the cord at the same time. His body arced down as he stretched out and grabbed the arm of the nearest lamppost. Spinning around it, he came to rest on top and looked down at the accident below, not letting himself think about the crazy stunt he'd just performed.

It was just as Wade had said; a car and a lorry had collided, the lorry driving over the bonnet of the car, and the car acting like a wedge had pushed the lorry onto its side. There was quite a crowd now gathered around. It looked like the drivers of both the car and lorry were shaken but unhurt. So where was the screaming coming from? Ghost glanced back at the lorry, and then he understood.

There was someone on the path underneath it. A woman was screaming, trying to get to the lorry, but was being held back by two men. Once again, without really thinking about what he was doing, Ghost leapt from the lamppost, landing with a crunch on the

roof of the flattened car. At the sound of his entrance, many in the crowd looked around.

"Out of the way," Grey-Ghost shouted in a deep, and what he had hoped was a confident tone. The crowd, many of them with their mouths agape, stood aside unthinking.

Ghost dived for the slender gap between the lorry and the path, slipping into the darkened recess. It took a moment for his eyes to adjust to the gloom, and then he found himself looking at the unconscious form of a man, only a few years older than himself. His foot was pinned beneath the wagon. Pulling him clear was out of the question.

Just then, the wagon slipped slightly, and the crowd on the outside screamed in panic. Ghost looked to see what was keeping the wagon from falling completely and squashing the two of them, and saw that it was resting on an ornate concrete litterbin. The bin was starting to crumble under the weight. If he didn't move now, they were both dead.

Ghost raised himself into a crouch, his back pressed firmly against the side of the wagon, his feet spread wide to take the weight. He had been wondering for several days now just how strong he had become. He was about to find out.

Slowly, Grey-Ghost started to straighten up, hands pressed against the cold steel of the trailer. Moments later, he had it clear of the bin so that he held all its weight on his back. It was agony. Every muscle screamed in protest as he pushed with all his might. Then he realised he could not push anymore. He could only raise it so far, and his position, with it resting against his back prevented him from going any further. He couldn't risk trying to turn the other way. One slip and that would be that. He was starting to despair, when he looked down and noticed that the man's leg was now free.

"Hey," Ghost yelled at the top of his voice, "someone drag this guy out."

A moment later, several faces appeared at the now bigger gap between the lorry and the path. They couldn't believe their eyes.

"Get him out of here. I can't hold this all day."

They seemed to falter for a moment, before one of them threw himself onto the path and crawled along on his belly until he reached the unconscious man. He grabbed two handfuls of his jacket and started to pull him out.

Grey-ghost closed his eyes and focussed beyond his screaming muscles. After what he reckoned was an eternity, someone called, "He's clear. What about you?"

That was a very good question. How was he going to get out? His whole body was starting to shake as he reached the limits of his energy. Blackness was creeping in at the edges of his vision.

"Everyone get clear," Ghost shouted with the last of

his strength. The crowd fell back, and moments later there was a terrible screeching sound and the lorry completely toppled over onto its side with a resounding crash that cracked the pavement.

As the dust settled, the people gathered around the truck unsure of what to do. The far off sounds of the emergency services reached their ears.

"They're too late," a woman in the crowd said, "he's dead, whoever he was."

Just then, there came the rending of metal, and the side of the wagon that was now pointing toward the night sky split open, and slowly, a masked man crawled his way out to stand on top. He looked unsteady on his feet.

Beneath his mask, Kyle grimaced through the pain. His body felt like one big bruise. From his high perch, he could see the approaching police. He had to get out of there while he was still able. Climbing back to the rooftops was out of the question. He toppled from the wagon to street level, and then took off up the nearest side street and away from the approaching emergency services.

Aching as he was, he was nowhere near top speed, but he was still fast enough to race past pedestrians who gawped at him, unsure of what they were seeing.

Several minutes later, Ghost was slowing to a halt in a darkened back alley. He slumped down onto the floor, his back resting against a grimy wall. Everything that had happened over the last hour came back to him in a rush. He realised he could have been killed several times over, and the thought of it made him retch. He just about lifted his mask clear of his mouth before throwing up all over the path.

When the heaving had stopped, Ghost climbed uneasily to his feet. Taking in his surroundings, Kyle realised he was only a few streets away from the Metro Cinema. Minutes later he hauled himself onto its roof and lay there breathing heavily.

"That was some job," a voice spoke just behind him.

Kyle groaned. Propping himself upon his elbows he looked around and saw both Billy and Wade standing there.

"You were awesome," Billy said with a wide grin on

his shiny face. "You actually picked an eighteen wheeled juggernaut up! Unbelievable. And the way you came bursting through the side of the wagon was amazing!"

"I could have done with some help," Kyle croaked as he looked from Billy to Wade. "Where were you?"

"He was ready to jump from the roof, Kyle," Billy said cutting in. "He had another line ready to get down to the street and everything."

"Is that right?"

Wade nodded. "It's time you were home in bed. You've done enough for one night."

"Does that mean we don't have to fight?" Ghost asked, his legs shaking as if they were made of rubber.

"It's you who wanted to do the fighting, remember?" Wade said with a small laugh.

"Yeah, sorry about that," he said awkwardly.

"Well, no damage done. We need to meet again. Tomorrow's Saturday. How does a trip to the museum sound?"

"No problem," Billy said eager to know what the stranger wanted. "Kyle?"

"Okay. Can we make it in the afternoon, though? The way I'm feeling right now, I think I'm going to spend the morning in the bath."

"Right," Wade said all business-like once more. "We'll iron out the details when I take you home."

"Oh," Ghost said surprised. "Do you have a car near here?"

"Not quite," Wade said as he pulled out what looked like some kind of remote control device from another pocket.

There was a sudden down blast of wind from overhead, and Kyle looked up at the sleek black silent helicopter that had appeared from nowhere.

"Who are you?" Ghost asked. He looked at Billy who was, grinning even wider than before.

"All in good time," Wade said, "all in good time."

14.

THE TWO-FACED MAN.

News of Grey-Ghost's appearance had spread like wild fire, and all of GateHaven was talking about nothing else. There were reporters from all the national newspapers scurrying around, tracking down any leads they could about the mysterious masked man who had suddenly appeared and then vanished without trace.

Kyle and Billy entered the museum after meeting up at the pre-arranged time. Even the museum seemed busier than normal for a Saturday.

"What time do we have to meet Wade?" Billy asked.

"He said for us to be in the Viking exhibit by two thirty." Kyle glanced at his watch. "It's after two now. We have a while before he arrives."

They idled away the time discussing in low voices the events of Friday night. Billy explained that in all the excitement he had forgotten his bike, and had to get up extra early that morning in order to sneak into town to retrieve it.

It occurred to them as they entered the Viking Hall that they did not even know what Wade looked like, so the less people in the hall the easier it would be to spot him.

Someone standing behind them cleared his throat.

"Excuse me," he said in a quiet voice, "I wonder if you could help me. I'm looking for someone. I believe he goes by the name of the Grey-Ghost?"

The boys spun around and found themselves looking at an old man. He was leaning heavily on a walking stick, and wore a dark grey suit with matching tie. His hair was short at the sides and he was bald on top. He wore steel-rimmed glasses, whose lenses were as thick as a slice of bread, and he sported a thick bushy moustache that was peppered with grey.

"Wade?" Kyle hissed between clenched teeth.

"The same," he said with a nod.

There was a pause, and then Billy said, "What's with the disguise?"

"Kyle has a secret identity, so why can't I?"

"You know my face," Kyle said sharply, "so why can't we know yours?"

"It's best that you don't," Wade replied.

"That seems unfair to me," Billy said. "I thought we were on the same team."

"And so we are. I just think it best to keep things as they are for now. It will cause fewer problems this way."

"In other words, you don't trust us," Billy said with contempt.

Wade grinned. "How clearly you put it."

"How do I know you can be trusted?" Kyle grimaced. "After last night, the whole city now knows about the Ghost. People are going to be looking for me. For all I know, you're going to hand me in the first chance you get."

"Is that what you really think? After last night, and

all we went through, don't you realise by now that I'm here to help you?"

Kyle shuffled his feet. "I suppose so. But all I seem to have done is draw attention to myself. That wasn't what I had in mind."

"You're missing the point," Wade said with a shake of the head. "You saved someone last night. That's the important thing to think about."

Wade tottered off toward the cabinets displaying the old clothing. The boys followed.

"I need your help," he said as he turned to face them. "Darius Crane is up to something. You, Kyle, seem connected to his plan in some way, so I'm hoping that the information I'm about to share will help you shed some light on things."

Billy looked into the cabinet. "You took it didn't you?"

Kyle looked from Billy to Wade. "Took what?"

Billy tapped on the glass. "I was here the other day, trying to figure out what had happened to Kyle in this room. The only difference I could see was that the belt was gone. I wasn't sure because they sometimes remove objects for cleaning. But you took it didn't you?"

"Yes," Wade said.

"What belt?" Kyle asked, bewildered.

"An old Viking belt with an engraving of Thor's hammer on the buckle. So far as I can tell," Wade said in a quiet voice, "Crane has been searching for this belt for years. Why it's so important to him is the puzzle I'm trying to solve."

Billy shrugged. "Crane's one of the richest men in the world, so it can't be for its value."

"Could it be more than just a belt?" Kyle asked. "Was something hidden inside it?"

"Hold on," Billy said, "Mr Crane is on the board of director's here. He is heavily into antiquities. My dad told me he has a private collection that would put this place to shame."

"But if Mr Crane has so much influence here at the museum," Kyle said, "why didn't he just take the belt? I'm sure no one's going to question someone of his importance."

"Yeah, that's right," Billy agreed. "Why go to all that trouble when he could have taken the thing any time he liked?"

Wade adjusted his glasses. "All I know is that when it was accidentally uncovered by a group of archaeologists, Crane saw to it that it came here first."

"How?" The boys asked together

"Crane has very influential friends. However, it would seem that no one else really knows the importance of this belt; otherwise, Crane wouldn't have gotten his hands on it so easily."

"But you've just handed it to him," Billy said.

Wade looked at Billy for a moment. "You're right. I did it to try to find out more of what was going on. I thought it was a belt and nothing more. It couldn't possibly present any sort of danger. But now I'm not so sure."

"What makes you think that?" Kyle asked.

"Because of you, Kyle."

"Me?"

"You said yourself that your strength appeared last Tuesday in this very building. That is too much of a coincidence, especially with Crane showing so much interest in you."

"What if it's the actual belt of Thor?" Billy shrugged.

Wade frowned. "What was that?"

Billy's eyes flicked from one to the other. "Well, Thor, as you probably both know was the God of Thunder, worshipped by the Vikings. He had a magical hammer. He was the only one who could lift it, and used it to control the weather. Thor could call down rain, snow, thunder, the whole works.

"The hammer could be thrown and would return to him. Thor also had a magical belt that doubled his strength. There was something else as well. Along with the belt, Thor wore a glove called Iron Grip. It protected him when he was channelling vast amounts of energy through his hammer."

"You make it sound like Thor actually existed," Kyle said with a grin.

"This doesn't make any sense," Wade interrupted. "Why is this belt so important to Crane? The man is only interested in one thing; power."

"You don't think..." Billy began, but then his voice trailed off as though he thought better of saying what he was thinking.

"Go on," Kyle urged.

"Well...you don't think that Crane is after the actual hammer of Thor?"

"I don't follow," Wade said with a shake of the head. "Even supposing the hammer actually existed, which is hardly unlikely, only Thor could lift it."

"What would happen if a normal person wore the belt and the glove at the same time?" Kyle asked innocently. "Do you think someone would be able to lift the hammer then?"

"Oh no," Billy blurted. "You don't suppose that's it? Suppose Mr Crane had both the belt and the glove. Would that give him the power to use the hammer?"

"Don't you think this is getting out of hand?" Wade said, almost laughing.

Billy glowered. "If you'd have asked me at the beginning of the week if it were possible for a teenager to pick up an eighteen wheeled truck, I'd have said you were mad."

"But you're talking about gods, and magic. Now I've seen a lot of strange things in my time," Wade said, peering at the boys over the top of his glasses, "but this is going too far. No, there has to be another reason why that belt is so important to him."

"But what?" Kyle said, sounding even more confused.

Wade shrugged. "I don't know, but if I'd have thought that my giving him the belt would enable Crane to wield a weapon that would allow him to control the weather, then I'd have kept it as far from the man as possible."

"Why?" Kyle asked.

"Because anyone who can control the weather patterns would rule the world." Wade was about to say something else, but before the words left his lips, he closed his mouth again, his eyes growing wide.

"What is it?" Both boys asked at the same time.

"Crane," Wade said, his own voice now strained. "I contacted him this morning. He thinks I'm keeping tabs on Kyle for him." He looked at Kyle, who was about to protest, but Wade held a hand up.

"It's all right, it's a chance for me to get closer, so I can see what Crane's up to. He was on board his private jet, heading for Norway for some reason."

"Norway?" Billy shouted. Other people in the hall looked around. "He could be after it right now. What are we going to do?"

"I'm going to have to go after him," Wade replied. "I just hope we're wrong about this."

"What do you want us to do?" Kyle asked, wide eyed.

"Nothing. Stay out of trouble, and most of all, keep out of sight. No Grey-Ghost excursions until I get back. Understand?"

Kyle shook his head. "No, I don't understand. What are you going on about?"

Wade looked at Billy. "Are you with me?"

Billy nodded. "I'll fill Kyle in with the details. How will you get there?"

"I have my own modes of transportation," Wade said,

already turning to leave. "I'll be in touch as soon as I've found out what's going on. Now remember, no super hero stuff."

The boys had returned to the restaurant, and while they sat over two glasses of coke, Billy explained what he thought Crane was doing.

"Crane must have found both the belt and the glove, and together they give him power over the hammer. That's why he's gone to Norway, to get his hands on it."

Kyle mulled this over as he took another swig from his glass.

"But it's still just guess work on our behalf isn't it? I mean, I'm not much when it comes to history, or in this case mythology, but this all seems too fantastic to be true." Kyle shook his head. "There is no proof that Thor ever existed."

"Well something made Wade take off in a bit of a hurry. What do you think we should do?" Billy asked.

"Well I don't know about you," Kyle said, a steely glint coming to his eye, "but I think it's time we started doing a little digging for information. What do you say?"

"What did you have in mind?"

"They've got internet access here at the museum haven't they?" Kyle asked as he looked around.

"Well, yeah," Billy replied. "There's an I.T. room here. All the history students use it."

"Great," Kyle said. "I reckon it's time we found out just exactly who Darius Crane is."

Billy hastily drained his glass. "Right then," he said, rising from his seat, "give me five minutes and I'll see what I can do."

Soon the boys had logged into a computer, accessed the Internet and were ready to type into the search engine the specific words for a search on Darius Crane. Moments later the search engine displayed its results. The screen was full of different site addresses they could visit. Billy scrolled down them, highlighting with the cursor the one he thought could offer the most information. It read; www.cranethemanthemyth.com.

"How about this one?" Billy asked over his shoulder to Kyle.

"Give it a try," Kyle urged.

The next couple of hours were spent pouring over information that told them plenty about the businessperson Darius Crane, but not about the private man. His forays into archaeological digs were shrouded in mystery. It was apparent that the man was exceedingly rich, and seemed very generous with his money, donating millions to charitable trusts. Crane appeared to have a great interest in global warming, famine in poor countries, and the preservation of endangered species.

When five o'clock came around, the two boys felt that their afternoon had uncovered little about this man. He appeared to be practically a saint. Surely, they had to be barking up the wrong tree.

They logged off the computer and made their way to the main hall. The crowds had thinned, and through the large windows, evening was drawing rapidly over the city outside like a heavy blanket.

By the time the boys were making their way home, it was dark outside. Neither of them saw a black van slip unnoticed into the milling traffic behind them.

15.

THE BAITED TRAP

Kyle yawned stiffly as he answered the front door that Sunday afternoon. Billy had turned up for their pre-arranged meeting, and as he let Billy in, Kyle noticed it was snowing. They went through to the living room, and as Billy took his seat, Kyle sat down heavily opposite him.

"What's the matter?" Billy asked.

Kyle yawned. "I don't know," he said. "I was feeling right as rain one minute, then the next thing, it's like something's taken my batteries out."

"When did this start?"

"Just before dinner," Kyle replied.

Just then, Cassie walked in, her arms full with dolls. She eyed Billy.

"It's all right Cass," Kyle said, "This is my friend Billy. Billy, this is Cassie."

Billy waved at the eight year old. Cassie smiled; her arms were too full to wave back.

"Can't you go and play upstairs?" Kyle asked her, "Billy and me have got a lot to talk about."

"Ooh, I wanted to play teachers in here," she pouted. Cassie suddenly yawned, dropping a couple of her dolls in the process. Billy rose from his seat, picked up the dolls and put them on top of the pile again.

"Okay then," Kyle said with a sigh, "but the moment you start bellowing, I'm throwing you out, understand?"

Cassie nodded vigorously and beamed. She crossed to a vacant seat and unloaded her dolls into it.

"Well," Kyle said in a quieter voice, sitting forward slightly, "Did you manage to find out anything else last night?"

Billy spent the next half hour going over all the web sites he had searched regarding Thor. There were quite a few sites dedicated to the Thunder God. They ranged from legendary tales and folklore, to sites about the popular American Marvel Comic.

The events surrounding the last days of Thor, and the other gods varied slightly with each telling. However, one thing they all seemed to agree on was that they were in a great battle called 'The Twilight of the Gods,' of which none survived.

"So the whereabouts of the hammer isn't even touched upon," Kyle said after listening to Billy's news.

Billy shook his head. "There's not one mention of it."

"That's not a lot of help." Kyle stifled yet another yawn. "So where do we go from here?"

"I suppose we wait for Wade to put in an appearance again. We've pretty much come up against a brick wall."

Kyle looked over at Cassie and was surprised to find her curled up on the chair fast asleep with all her dolls around her.

"Is she okay?" Billy asked following his gaze.

"Yeah, she's just getting over a bad cold. Mum says

she hasn't been sleeping very well, so I guess she's napping whenever she can."

Billy glanced out the window and noticed that the snowing had stopped.

"Weird weather we're having today," he said more to himself, but Kyle had heard him.

"Do you reckon it's got something to do with all this global warming we keep hearing about?" Kyle asked as he too looked up from his seat.

"Probably," Billy said. "I'd better get going before it decides to hailstone or something. You're not planning on going out as the Ghost any time soon are you?"

Kyle shook his head. "Not feeling like this I'm not."

"Well I'll see you at school in the morning," Billy said as he stepped out into the cool breeze. "Maybe there's a note waiting for you in your school locker."

"I hope so," Kyle replied. "I can't stand all this waiting for something to happen."

Billy grinned. "I know what you mean; I just hope that Wade has had more luck than we have."

The first thing he was aware of was the coppery taste of blood in his mouth. It was with great effort that he opened his heavy lidded eyes. Everything was blurred. He ached from the tips of his toes to the roots of his hair. Realisation then hit him that he was tied to a chair. He flexed against his bonds but it was useless.

His mask was gone too, but he had more pressing problems that demanded his attention. Slowly, everything swam into focus. He was strapped into a steel chair. There were metal bindings at his wrists.

He glimpsed the cloth of his body suit and was surprised to find it singed in places. There was a light directly over his head that spilled its dim glow in a perfect circle on the floor. Darkness lay beyond the pool of light, and the place felt huge, cavernous.

There was the sound of a bolt scraping back, and a large door opening. A moment later the door slammed shut, the clanging echoing through the vastness of the room.

Footsteps were coming closer. Three, no, four people heading his way. Darius Crane approached, flanked on either side by bodyguards roughly the same size as young killer whales. They were dressed in Armani, and each pointing the business end of a gun at him.

"Forgive me if I don't get up," Wade quipped, "I'm a little tied up at the moment."

Crane nodded. "After tonight, there will be no need for you to ever get up again."

"Sounds like you have some plans for me."

"The plans are only short term, Mr Wade. Nothing for you to worry about. I must say I am disappointed. I was expecting more of a challenge from you, yet you blundered into my trap like a rank amateur."

Wade kept his expression blank.

Crane turned to his guards. "Leave us," he said.

The three bodyguards strode away into the shadows. Wade took note that he did not hear the door open again.

"I want you to know that you've failed," Crane said. "I know that you only agreed to assist me from the beginning so you could keep tabs on me. Why do you think I chose you? I wanted you close so I could keep track of *you*. Your network of informants was easy to access. If you have money, Mr Wade, you have power."

"How long have you known?"

Crane grinned like a shark. "Long enough. I could have taken the belt at any time, after all, I own most of the museum at GateHaven. Didn't it seem odd to you that I enlist a man of your talents to go to all those lengths to get something that I could have taken at any time?"

Wade grinned back. "Well you've sure played me for a fool."

"You certainly are a man of mystery, and your reputation among the criminal underworld is legendary." Crane circled the chair, like a vulture circling its prey. "So it seemed the easiest thing for me to do was to have you work for me. It also helped the fact that you are the best at what you do. When that bumbling Swiss archaeology team stumbled upon the belt by accident, you were the obvious choice to verify it's authenticity for me."

Wade laughed aloud. It echoed eerily though the darkness.

"I must be getting too old for this game not to see that

one coming," he said, and laughed again.

"But what about young McKinley? How does he all fit into this?" Crane asked.

"He's nothing to do with this at all. I've watched him. It's just some kind of weird coincidence him showing up when he did."

"Ah, but you would say that wouldn't you?" Crane said smirking. "That's why I paid him a little visit the other day at the hospital. No, you're wrong about that young man. He is very much involved in this, and after Monday I'll know just how involved he really is."

"What have you got in mind for him?" Wade tried to keep the concern out of his voice.

"I'd worry more about my own skin than some interfering school kid if I were you."

Crane glanced at his watch. "Oops, is that the time? Well I would love to stay and chat, but I have a pressing engagement in GateHaven. If you'll excuse me. It was nice knowing you Mr wade, you've certainly kept me... entertained."

"Wait," Wade cried as Crane stepped out of the circle

of light.

"Yes?" Crane said after a moment. He stayed beyond the reach of the lamplight.

"I don't even know what it was you hit me with," Wade said, trying to buy more time.

"That's all right," Crane replied as he started to move away, "the rest of the world will feel exactly the same way when I introduce them to my new toy. Goodbye Mr Wade."

Wade looked around frantically, trying to think of a way out. Then he heard them, heavy footsteps heading his way. They didn't sound as if they were in any hurry; after all, he wasn't going anywhere.

"Some days it just doesn't pay to get out of bed," Wade said between gritted teeth as the footsteps drew ever closer.

16.

UNEXPECTED TRIP

Monday morning was soon upon Kyle and Billy. Kyle, for some reason felt restless. After Mr Miller had called the register, he asked for silence.

"Who's a lucky bunch of so-and-so's then?" There were raised heads and questioning looks.

"Today, this class is going on another field trip, courtesy of Mr Darius Crane." Mr Miller paused for a moment for murmuring to die down. "It's all been arranged over the weekend. Mr Crane was apparently worried you hadn't got the best out of the visit last week for obvious reasons, so this is just his way of apologising."

"Who are we to argue with him, Sir," Kyle drawled.

The class burst into laughter.

Mr Miller ignored the last comment. "All mobile phones are to be left at school because Mr Crane will be there in person, and it's to minimize publicity. As you know, your parents have signed consent forms previously, but we still rang them over the weekend for their permission for you to go. A lot of hard work has gone into arranging this, so I hope you'll appreciate it by behaving today."

"My folks never said anything," Dave Thomas said loudly. There was a muttering of agreement among the class.

"That's because they were asked not to say anything in case you told someone other than your family before you went on the trip. It's all to do with security for Mr Crane, and we don't want a media circus down there, do we? Now have a good time, and for goodness sake, try and learn something won't you?"

Five minutes later, the class trooped out single file to theschool gates. The coach was already there, complete with Miss Beechum. Billy had entered the coach first, and as Kyle passed him on his way to sit at the back, they looked at each other and shrugged.

Miss Beechum climbed the steps and addressed the class once they were seated.

"Well that's all of you accounted for," she began with a nod. "Now all we have to do is wait for Mr Lamb."

Just as the words had left her mouth, so Mr Lamb turned the corner of the schoolyard. As he climbed the steps into the coach, he looked out of breath. After a quick word with Miss Beechum, he took his seat as the coach pulled away.

Before long, they were pulling up outside the museum. Mr Blake was already there to greet them. "Have we met before?" Mr Blake asked with a wide grin. There was a ripple of laughter. "Welcome once again. I don't know how much you've been told, but Mr Crane has generously donated the use of this Museum today."

"It's true then," Mr Lamb croaked, he seemed to be suffering with a sore throat, "We're the only ones here today?"

"Absolutely," Miles nodded. "Apart from the usual

staff, you have the run of the place. It is now nine thirty," Miles said glancing at his watch. "At twelve thirty you will all be escorted to lunch in the restaurant. Once you have eaten, the rest of the afternoon is yours until it is time to return you to school. Is everything clear?"

There was a nodding of heads.

"Great, I'll leave you to it then." With a smile and a wave at some of the faces he knew, Mr Blake made for the staircase.

"Right then," Miss Beechum piped up, "the girls will go with me while the boys will accompany Mr Lamb. I want you to visit the Battalion exhibit to make sure you got all the relevant information, and then I want you to pick one of the other halls, study its contents, and then for homework, write a brief essay about it."

There was a general groan from everyone.

An hour later Kyle finally caught up with Billy, who was scribbling notes on some paper regarding the skeletal remains of a velociraptor. Kyle was on his own, having shaken off his group by pretending to go to the toilet.

"This is a bit too coincidental, don't you think?" He asked when he was sure no one else was listening.

Billy looked up. "I'm trying not to think about it," he said nervously. "What do you think he's up to?"

Kyle shrugged. "It could be nothing. We could be reading too much into all of this. But it would help if we could find out what Wade is doing".

"I wonder if anything's happened to him," Billy muttered. "What if he went after Mr Crane and they got him?"

Just then, Miss Beechum started calling everyone through to the foyer. As the whole class congregated, there was a flurry of activity by the front doors. The next moment Darius Crane himself came bustling through, flanked on either side by bodyguards.

"This is getting worse all the time," Billy moaned. He glanced at Kyle, who to his surprise was looking suddenly pale.

A commanding voice cut through the bustling chatter of the foyer.

"Thank you for joining us today," Mr Crane said,

extending his arms in welcome. "The further education of our future generations is something very precious to me. It bothered me greatly the other day that your field trip here was blighted by the theft of the Sapphire Spider.

"So think of this museum as yours for the day. You can complete your studies, but feel free to wander the corridors, where you may make new discoveries that will broaden your horizons."

There was a round of applause from the gathered crowd. Kyle on the other hand kept his hands jammed in his pockets.

"Also," Mr Crane added, flashing his perfect teeth for effect, "I would like to take this moment to thank Kyle McKinley for trying to help out last Tuesday, and I have a special presentation for him. I do hope he's with us this morning." Crane scanned the faces before him.

Heads turned in Kyle's direction, and with great reluctance, he raised his hand.

"Ah there you are. Come and join me, lad. Don't be shy."

Kyle picked his way through his classmates, trying

to keep his face neutral. His legs felt like water. He was shivering, and it wasn't from fear.

"Kyle," Crane said, beaming once he had joined him and faced the class. "On behalf of Mr Ibun Khan, I would like to present you with a cheque made out to your school to the value of twenty thousand pounds to update its computer facilities. And from myself, season tickets to the Haven Harriers, your favourite team I believe. I have a box there, which is at your families' disposal, of course. These are only small tokens, I know, but please accept them with our deepest thanks."

Kyle tried to show some sign of enthusiasm as his classmates and assembled museum staff broke into rapturous applause. The best he could muster was a somewhat sickly smile.

"Kyle," said Miss Beechum from the front of the crowd, "perhaps you'd like to say something?"

"Uh, sure," Kyle stammered. "On behalf of the school, I'd like to say thanks very much. As for the tickets, well I really didn't do anything."

"Is he always this modest?" Crane asked Miss Beechum

with a hearty laugh, clapping Kyle on the shoulder.

"Not usually, no." she replied honestly.

Kyle went rigid, and then slumped forward as if he was going to pass out. Crane reacted like lightning. He lowered Kyle to the floor then beckoned one of his aides over. The gorilla in Armani swept Kyle into his arms and then proceeded to make his way through the crowd to the back of the hall.

"Where is he taking him?" Miss Beechum asked as she started to follow.

Mr Crane stepped in front of her and blocked her way. "It's quite all right," he said. "There is a first aid room just off the foyer. My aide is taking him there to make him more comfortable. I assure you that Kyle is in safe hands. Eugene is medically trained, but it's all right, since we're fairly sure we know what ails the lad."

"What *is* the matter with him?" Mr Lamb was about to side step Crane and see for himself.

"Haven't you been told?" Mr Crane asked eyebrows arched in surprise. "It all stems from the gas last week. Apparently Kyle has a rare blood group, and the sedative in the gas affects this blood group more than your average 'O' or 'A' groups for instance. It remains in their system longer for some reason, and in moments of excitement, it can make him light-headed. A strong cup of tea will put him right, mark my words."

"How do you know about this blood disorder?" Lamb asked his eyes narrowed.

"I have ownership in this museum you know," Crane shrugged, "and I have to admit that my legal people looked into it when the kids were knocked out by the gas. For all we knew, we were looking at…"

"Legal action against you and the museum," Mr Lamb said cutting across him. "That's what the school contribution is really all about isn't it?"

"Well I wouldn't have put it like that, but we have to protect our interests as well as look out for the kids well being. It's simply good business."

"I still want to have a look at him," Mr Lamb said in a tone that said he wouldn't take no for an answer.

"Very well. We'll go together if you like."

When they reached the first aid room, they were

surprised to find Kyle sat up on an examination table, looking groggy but awake.

"There you go," Mr Crane beamed, "give him a chance to get his breath back and he'll be right as rain again."

"How are you feeling?" Miss Beechum asked tentatively.

"Just a bit giddy," Kyle said. "I'm more embarrassed than anything, conking out like that."

"Well if you're sure," Mr Lamb said, his face lined with worry.

Just then, Mr Crane's Armani clad aide spoke. For a man his size, he had remained surprisingly inconspicuous in such a small room.

"Excuse me sir, but Kyle really should be getting some rest."

"Of course," Crane boomed, "you know best, Eugene. Shall we?" and he ushered the teachers out of the room.

I'm afraid I must leave you now," Crane said. "I have a pressing engagement, so if you will excuse me." He nodded then made for the staircase, another Armani clad gorilla following like an obedient terrier.

Once out of earshot Mr Crane turned to his aide.

"It seems my suspicions are confirmed, Alexander. I want the boy brought to the central gallery in ten minutes."

"And what about phase two?" Alexander enquired.

"Put it into operation once I'm with the boy."

Crane proceeded down a corridor off the main stairway and stopped before a heavy looking door. His eyes fell on a boy in school uniform just a little further along the corridor, engrossed in a cabinet housing Egyptian pottery. He reached in his pocket and withdrew a small brass key. It was the only one for that particular door.

The room beyond was small and sparsely furnished with oak panelled walls. There was a wooden crate on the desk, about the size of a large suitcase. Crane smiled grimly. With case in hand, all he had to do is slip down the back stairs unseen. Then it would be time for McKinley.

Billy had been coming back from his dad's office, where he had gone to tell him what had happened to

Kyle. He was making his way to the foyer when he heard Mr Crane's voice around the corner. Flattening himself against the wall, Billy edged closer until he could clearly hear what was being said. Crane was obviously talking about Kyle.

Then Billy heard footsteps coming his way, and he raced on cat feet back down the corridor. Realising he couldn't get out of sight in time, he skidded to a halt before a display cabinet and pretended to be interested in its contents. Mr Crane rounded the corner the next instant, coming to a stop before a small door.

He seemed to look Billy's way before pulling out a key unlocking the door and disappearing inside.

Billy slowly made his way to the door. Taking a second to glance down the corridor, he pressed his ear to the wood. He couldn't hear a thing. Why did Crane want Kyle taken to the main hall where the robbery had taken place? Moreover, how could Billy get in there without being seen?

A thought occurred to him, and Billy raced for the stairs.

17.

A LESSON IN HISTORY

After making a brief stop, Billy rode the lift up to the fourth floor. As the doors opened, he surged out into the corridor, running its full length until he came to a dead end. There was a solitary door in front of him, and on it was a small sign that read;

CLEANER

Fishing inside his blazer, he withdrew a small key that he had taken from the rack of keys in his Dad's office a few minutes earlier. He entered the cupboard and locked it behind him. It took him a moment to find the light switch.

The cupboard was crammed with cleaning utensils.

Mops and buckets lined one wall, along with an industrial vacuum cleaner and a floor polisher. Alongside these were boxes of detergents and soaps for the toilets.

He pushed the boxes aside, exposing the back wall. Set into this wall was a wire mesh grille. He hooked his fingers into the mesh and pulled. The whole grille came loose leaving a gaping maw in the wall. Beyond was the museum's old ventilation system.

Billy had come across this particular opening at the tender age of nine. The labyrinth of ventilation ducting that spread through the walls and ceilings of the museum was like a rabbit warren of secret tunnels. It had been his favourite place to play when he was a kid.

As he pushed himself head first into that dark oblong in the wall he realised just how much bigger he was at the grand old age of thirteen. He reached a junction in the venting. Pausing to brush away the cobwebs tangled in his hair, he tried to remember which way would take him to the hall.

He was aware of the coolness of the floor tile pressed

against his cheek. Kyle sat up, and was surprised to find himself in the exhibition hall the robbery had taken place last week.

Kyle became aware of someone moving at the far end of the room. It was Darius Crane. He was on his own for once, and was carrying a crate. Kyle's eyes raked the room. All the security doors were in place. Even the one that he had damaged had been replaced. The various displays were empty; all the exhibits removed from the hall.

"How are we feeling?" Crane asked pleasantly as he stopped and placed the box down by his feet.

"What am I doing here?"

"We both know what you've gone through in the last week. Just as we know there is a connection between us. Remember that feeling in the hospital the other day when we made skin contact?"

Kyle blinked. "I don't know what..."

"Oh come now," Crane snorted, "don't insult my intelligence, young man."

"I... I just felt a little giddy, that's all," Kyle stammered.

He began to look for a way out.

Crane grinned then stooped and rummaged around in the crate for a moment. When he withdrew, upon his right hand was a glove. It was of dark, cracked leather, its knuckles covered in iron bolt heads.

"Do you know what this is?"

Kyle blinked. "Iron Grip."

"Very good," Crane said. "Then do you know what this is?"

Mr Crane undid the buttons on his jacket. As the jacket swung open to reveal shirt and tie, Kyle's eyes were drawn to the item around Crane's waist.

"The belt of Thor," Kyle said automatically. There was a sudden ringing in his ears, like a tiny voice babbling incoherently.

"I have one other item in the box. Would you like to see it?"

In one swift movement, Crane withdrew it, holding it overhead. The lights in the room flickered.

It was bigger than Kyle had imagined. The head of the hammer was about four times as big as a house brick. He couldn't tell what the hammerhead was made from, but it looked like granite, shot through with spidery veins of red and gold.

The handle was three feet in length, wrapped in sheep's wool and bound in place by a latticework of coarse leather. The handle ended in a thong, which was looped around Crane's wrist.

"This belt, glove, and hammer were once the property of the most powerful Norse God of all."

"You're mad to believe that," Kyle said. "Thor didn't really exist. There's no proof to suggest that he did. It's just folklore."

"So the boy needs proof," Crane said, grinning.

He held the hammer out at arms length, his brow knitted in concentration. The sky that was visible through the domed skylight overhead grew suddenly dark. There was an enormous clap of thunder, and then the heavens opened up. Rain was hitting the glass as though it was trying to shatter it.

"Now, watch this," Crane hissed.

The wind picked up, and the very walls of the museum

shuddered as the storm raged outside. What little strength Kyle had remaining, evaporated. Everything slid out of focus, and he slipped into the welcoming darkness for a while.

"Wake up little man; you've had a busy morning."

Kyle tried to focus through the fog that smothered his thoughts. He sat up with great effort. "How long have I been out?" he rasped.

"A little over a minute."

"What have you done to me?"

Crane's eyes were bright with success. "Well, I'm only surmising, but from what I can ascertain, I've channelled your energy through the hammer."

"I don't understand." Kyle felt numb. He looked up at the dome again to see the sky relatively cloud free.

"Let me tell you a tale that will both thrill and amaze," Crane said theatrically, as if addressing a hidden audience. "Tell me Kyle, have you ever heard of a man called Adolf Hitler?"

"Um, yeah. He led Germany into the Second World

War. He was a madman."

"You misunderstand him," Crane said as he smoothed his goatee thoughtfully. "Hitler was a man with a vision. He saw Germany as the pure race, fit to rule the world, with him as absolute ruler. In order to achieve his ambitions, Hitler needed power. But conventional means of power was not enough."

"How do you mean?" Kyle asked.

"When Hitler was a young man he visited Vienna. Whilst there, he came across an artefact on show in a treasure house called 'The Spear of Destiny.' This relic was supposed to be the spearhead that pierced the side of Jesus Christ whilst he was on the cross. Hitler is quoted to have said that he went into a trance standing before the spear, and it showed him his future.

"Once he had risen to power, Hitler had his army march into Vienna and seize the spear, where it was taken to Nuremberg. A year later Germany invaded Poland, and so began the Second World War."

"I was right," Kyle grimaced. "The man was mad."

"Hitler was heavily into antiquities," Crane went on

as if Kyle hadn't interrupted. "It was through his passion for history that he became obsessed for finding the things that legends are made of. Hitler's men started combing the globe for items of 'power,' The Arc of the Covenant, the Holy Grail, King Arthur's sword Excalibur, and the hammer of Thor. He recruited the finest archaeologists and historians to aid him in his search. Among those persuaded was my Father."

Kyle gaped. "Your dad? But he was British. What was he doing working with the enemy?"

"My Father had been a flyer with the RAF. During one of his missions, his plane was shot down and he was taken as a prisoner of war. Father had studied archaeology at Oxford, and this came to the attention of the SS, Hitler's elite troops. They gave him a choice; work for them or face a firing squad. Being a survivor, he naturally chose to aid them in their search, hoping that later he could find the means to escape.

"When I was no older than ten I stumbled across a hidden room at our country estate in Buckinghamshire. I was playing. I must have accidentally sprung a hidden lever or something, for the next thing I know, the rear wall of the cupboard opened to reveal a small room beyond."

A brief smile played across the billionaire's lips. "Over the next few years I found out how my Father had built from scratch one of the biggest industrial empires in the world."

"How?"

"Simple," Crane said with a shrug and a grin, "he stole the ideas."

Kyle frowned. "Who from?"

"Why the Nazi's of course. While he was relic hunting for the Fuhrer, he was secretly taking notes of everything that he saw. Father had also duped the Nazi's into thinking that he was now co-operating with them of his own free will."

"How do you know all this?"

"Father kept extensive journals of everything he did, everything he saw. So all the while, Father was building his own future as Hitler's began to crumble. When the war was over and Germany lay in ashes, Father was free to realise his own empire.

"He all but forgot about the documents relating to historical finds he had gathered for the enemy. I read them avidly, but was disappointed to find that most of the digs had come to nothing. However, among the worthless paperwork was a small book, relating to the legend of a magical glove that had once belonged to Thor himself. I could glean from Father's writings that he had thought it to be another waste of time.

"The book turned out to be a record of an expedition from the turn of the twentieth century. A band of Norwegian archaeologists set out to discover the whereabouts of the hammer. The record went on to say that the expedition met with disaster, an avalanche, killing all but one of the team. He turned out to be one of the hired help, a digger whose knowledge of the region was second to none.

"The actual book though, had belonged to one of the main party who had financed the find. This local chap had retrieved it from the dead man before returning home to get help. The very last entry in the book goes on about the sighting of a large glove buried deep within the ice. I can only assume that disaster struck before the team could confirm their find.

"I became obsessed with the idea of finding the glove. I don't know to this day, why I did, but something about this tale spoke to me."

Kyle watched as a wide range of emotions struggled to break through Crane's mask-like expression.

"When I went to Oxford," Crane continued, "I studied in the fields that I was passionate about, much to Father's displeasure. He told me I was wasting my time, but allowed me to follow my dreams, insisting that one day I would learn a valuable lesson in life. Nevertheless, I financed several attempts to unearth the glove.

"My early digs met with disaster But I was not about to give in, and at last my patience was rewarded. When I removed it from the ice, it was as though it had been made only yesterday. The glove felt warm to the touch, like it was alive."

"Alive?"

Crane nodded his eyes over bright. "But the real

surprise was when I put the glove on. It was as if someone was whispering in my ear, a restless voice, trying to tell me something. I couldn't fully understand what it was saying, but eventually I worked out that it wanted to be joined with the others."

"What others?" Kyle asked, wondering if the voice Crane heard was the one that he could hear now.

"The glove wanted to be with the belt and the hammer. There is some kind of connection between them." Crane's eyes went wide. "And then I saw it at once. My destiny mapped out before me. The glove could guide me to the belt, which would in turn lead me to the hammer.

"Once the glove was in my possession, it was almost as if it was telling me where to look for the belt. However, the area it pointed to was vast. The glove wouldn't work properly for me. I could wield the strength in it, but something was missing."

"I'd imagine it was because the glove wasn't yours to begin with," Kyle said shakily.

"You're closer to the truth than you know," Crane nodded. "But in the meantime, my Father was pressuring me to take a keener interest in the family business. This I did, just to keep the old man quiet. But then my parents decided to go and get themselves killed in a bloody plane crash."

"You don't seem too upset," Kyle said.

"With them gone," Crane continued, "my expeditions were put on the back burner as I took control of my father's empire. To begin with, Father's lawyers and close business colleagues guided me, but I am a fast learner if nothing else, and within two years, I had the businesses running the way I wanted. It was then that I could continue my searches for the belt and the hammer, but they proved to be more elusive than the glove, despite it acting as a sort of detector. Though of course I now know why that was."

"You do?" Kyle asked, eyeing Crane shrewdly.

"It's because of you Kyle, and your connection to this hammer."

"What connection?"

"The hammer belongs to you," Crane said simply.

"What?"

"Where do you think your strength came from? It happened last week when you were in close proximity to the belt. When Mr Wade reported to me that he had been chased by a school boy, I naturally put two and two together."

"But why would you think that?" Kyle asked, not seeing the logic in Crane's assumption.

"Because for some time now, the glove has been for want of a better word, 'pulling' me toward GateHaven. It's been trying to return home. That's why I was getting conflicting readings from it when I was trying to locate the belt and hammer.

"I was just too keen to find out what was attracting the glove's attention to this city, so I surmised that sending the belt here, once it had been found, would help accelerate my search for whatever it was. I was no doubt proven right, for here you are before me."

"I ... don't know what to say," Kyle stammered. It felt like this was happening to somebody else and not him.

Crane's face grew serious. "It was easy to find out the school that had visited that day, and when I met you at the hospital I made sure I was wearing the belt. I could feel it's excitement in my head as I entered your room. It merely confirmed my suspicions about you. But I have to admit that even I was taken unawares as to what occurred when we shook hands."

"I ... I felt suddenly weak," Kyle said.

"I know," Crane said, "because I siphoned your energies through the belt, making me stronger. Touching you was like getting a charge from a battery. I knew that I would need both the belt and the glove to even lift the hammer, let alone use its untapped magic. Then with my little experiment just a while ago, I find that I can channel the full power of the hammer whilst absorbing your strength at the same time.

"It's like you're the missing part of the puzzle, Kyle!"

Kyle took a step back. "Even if that's true, I'm not about to let you use me."

Crane looked Kyle right in the eye. "You're nothing more than a power cell to drain at my leisure. Which leads me to my final realisation ... that you must somehow be a descendant of Thor himself?"

This last statement hit Kyle like a slap in the face. "You mean ..." he started, but couldn't get all the words out.

Crane nodded. "It's the only logical explanation. How else can you explain your strength? Or that the hammer is trying to communicate to you as we speak?"

"Y-you can hear it too?"

"No. I can feel it. My understanding has been largely down to guesswork." Crane's voice was full of resentment.

"Well I can't understand what it's trying to tell me," Kyle said truthfully, "so I can't be related to Thor."

"I'm right about you boy," Crane hissed through clenched teeth, "and with your help I'm going to achieve my goal."

"And what's that?"

"The world, boy. I want the world!"

Kyle had heard enough. If it was true what Crane had told him, he couldn't even be in the same room with this mad man. Moving quicker than he had ever done before, Kyle leapt upwards, his strength carrying him into the criss-cross framework in the roof. Crane screamed after him, and as Kyle found his footing, he looked down at the billionaire.

Crane was holding the hammer out before him with both hands, his face a mask of concentration. Kyle panicked. Crane was trying to absorb his strength again, and if Kyle weakened suddenly and fell from this height, then it was all over.

However, nothing was happening, and as Kyle looked down again he could see the frustration on Crane's features. Kyle felt a surge of relief. He was obviously out of range. Crane had to be right next to him, or better yet touching Kyle for the leaching process to occur.

Crane reached into his pocket for his phone. He speed- dialled a number. From way up on his perch, Kyle heard Crane say, "Phase two," before replacing the phone in his pocket.

Suddenly from outside there came the sound of breaking glass and gunfire. Screams echoed through the vast hallways beyond the locked door, and the sound of running feet slapped the cold floor tiling.

"What's going on?" Kyle shouted down.

"An insurance policy on my part," Crane boomed up into the rafters. "Either you do as I say, or your little friends out there are going to suffer. The choice is yours, young man. Don't make me blast you down, or even worse, hurt one of your school Chums."

"What do you mean 'blast'?" Kyle couldn't help asking as he scrabbled for a way out of this mess.

"Why this," Crane said, and pointed the hammerhead first at where Kyle was perched.

Then all hell broke loose.

18.

LEAP OF FAITH

"Almost got you that time, boy!" Crane rasped, his sweaty face alight with malice.

Kyle released his hold, dropping to the carpeting thirty feet below, just as a blast of lightning hit the exact spot on which he had been perched. Sparks rained down on his head as he went into a roll, coming up in a crouch behind a glass cabinet.

"You're running out of time and space, Kyle." Crane advanced slowly, the air crackling around the hammerhead. "One call to my men outside and one of your little friends will be made to suffer."

The cabinet exploded as lightning lashed outward

from the hammer again. Kyle threw himself backwards as a hail of glass shards flew at him. He avoided most of it, but one deadly splinter caught his cheek, leaving a wicked gash.

Reaching forward, Kyle seized the cabinet, and he hefted it into the air at Crane, but he swatted it aside as if he was playing cricket.

"Nice try boy," Crane laughed, "but I'm not about to be stopped by flying furniture."

Crane reached into his pocket. He was going for his phone again. Kyle leapt forward, barrelling into him and sending him flying. The phone went skittering across the polished floor. Kyle tracked its progress, disentangled himself from Crane and took off after it, already feeling weaker just by touching Crane. Fumbling fingers clutched the phone and Kyle crushed it to pieces.

Kyle leapt for the steelwork again. He struggled to pull himself into a small recess between girder and ceiling that he had not noticed before. A blast of lightning hit the roof right beside where Kyle lay in shadow. This spurred him into moving. He edged his way along the steel beam.

"You think you're clever don't you, destroying my phone like that," Crane shouted into the rafters. There was another blast of lightning, but Kyle was some distance from it.

Kyle was trying to figure out his next move, when he could have sworn that someone called his name. There it was again, directly in front of him. Kyle risked a peek over the edge. Tucked just underneath the beam by the wall was a ventilation grille.

Moreover, behind the grille was the worried face of Billy Blake. Kyle shot a quick look toward Crane, who was striding the other way, and shimmied along until he was at the wall.

"Billy," he hissed, "what the hell do you think you're doing?"

"Trying to find out what's going on," Billy replied. "Kyle, you've got to get out there."

"I can't. There's no way I can make it to the door before he cuts me down."

"What about getting out through the glass in the roof?"

"No good, I'll be an open target for him. Hang on, what about the vent system you're in?"

Billy shook his head. "Not a chance, I only just fit in here myself, and you're a lot broader than me."

A blast of lightning from the other side of the hall made the two boys jump.

"Some men have stormed the building," Kyle blurted. "They're Crane's goons. He has them here to ensure that I co-operate. I can't let him get to me. If he does, he says he'll have the full power of the hammer. H-he reckons I'm related to Thor."

Billy nodded. "I know, I've heard everything. How are you holding up?"

Kyle shrugged. "There's a pattern forming. If he gets too close, he can absorb my strength. But I reckon that when he creates weather with it I start to feel really tired. Either way that hammer is affecting me somehow."

"Tired? Are you sure?" Billy asked.

"Yeah, I think so, why?"

"I'm not sure," Billy said, chewing his lip.

Kyle started. "He's coming back this way. Look mate,

whatever you're planning to do, just do it fast, ok?"

Kyle slid out from the top of the girder and unexpectedly dropped to the floor below.

"So what do you want from us?" Miles Blake asked the masked man before him. They had been herded into hall one, school kids and museum staff alike. Each was as scared as the next as they were surrounded by masked gunmen.

"Which one of you is Miles Blake?"

"That would be me," Mr Blake said.

"Is everyone accounted for?"

Mr Blake did a quick head count of staff and then looked over at Miss Beechum and Mr Lamb for help. Mr Lamb took a step forward.

"Everyone's here," he said hoarsely.

Mr Blake's eyes swept across the frightened faces of the children, who stood huddled together like lost sheep. He smiled reassuringly. However, the smile faded when he could not see Billy. He looked back at Mr Lamb, alarm rising in him.

"Everyone's here," Miles said quickly, "now what's going on?"

The gunman approached Mr Lamb and Mr Blake.

"Follow me into the next room." He beckoned and two of his men stepped forward.

"I'll get straight to the point," the apparent leader said as the door closed. "Darius Crane is the one we're after. All I ask of you two is to keep your staff and pupils quiet. Co-operate and you will all leave here alive. Is that understood?"

The curator and teacher nodded.

"Good. As long as we understand one another, everything will go swimmingly. Now if you could return to the rest of the crowd in the other hall."

The masked leader watched the two men leave under guard and then turned to one of his men.

"Give it ten minutes, and then contact Mr Crane. It won't be long before the law surrounds us. I just hope he knows what he's doing."

All the display cabinets had turned to matchsticks.

Debris littered the floor. There were scorch marks on the walls. Among all this, two figures circled each other warily.

Both of them bloodied, but Crane looked the healthier. The sound of police sirens wailed outside the museum.

"The cavalry have arrived," Crane smirked. It's a pity they're too late." He gestured toward Kyle, and a sudden blast of ice cold wind swept the boy off his feet and slammed him head first into a pillar. He hit the floor hard, plaster raining down on him.

Crane strode over to Kyle's limp form and picked him up with his free hand. "Give in," Crane said, his face serious. "Together you and I can reshape this world into a better place. War and famine will become things of the past. We can make the deserts fertile. No one need go hungry again, I will see to that. I'll be the voice of reason in this world gone mad!"

Once back at the cupboard Billy's plan was formed. He had to get to the roof. He went to the door, stooped and looked through the keyhole at the corridor on the other side. It was clear. Billy unlocked it and slipped outside. His best bet was the fire exit stairs.

Billy crept along the carpeted corridor until he came to the door leading to the stairwell. Opening the door at the top of the stairs, he peered cautiously out into the corridor beyond. At the far end stood one of the men in black. He had his back to Billy and was peering out of a window, at what was going on in the street below.

Billy slipped quietly through the door and rounded the corner out of sight. This end of the corridor was thankfully empty. The door to the roof looked just like any other in the corridor save for the fact that it had a digital combination pad for a lock. Billy knew the code and punched it in.

It was now that he thanked his lucky stars that he had spent time wandering around the museum with the security guards. From here, it was one more flight of steps and another door and he would be on the roof.

He took the steps two at a time and stopped before the door. It was similar to the previous one, complete with keypad, except this door was steel plated. Billy punched in the combination, turned the handle and the door swung outwards. A cold wind blew at him, chilling him and cooling the sweat on his face.

Billy looked out across the roof. It was vast and dotted with skylights that capped the various halls inside. The dome of the central hall took pride of place, its shatterproof glass glittering in the dying afternoon sun.

The police would be stationed on the front steps, and that was directly in front of him. Billy gathered all his strength and sprinted for the far end of the roof. He skidded to a halt at the rail that ran around the roofs perimeter.

Hopping up onto the ledge he peered over into the street. Police, ambulance and fire crews swarmed around like busy worker ants below. Billy waved frantically and caught a police officers attention. The uniformed man pointed up at him and all heads swung his way.

Billy started yelling down to the street below. The high wind, plus the height he was at was making it hard for him to make them understand. He would just have to yell louder.

The roof door had banged ominously open and booted feet were crunching across the gravel toward him.

"You, boy!" an angry voice yelled over the rising wind.

Billy turned in time to see one of the men in black rushing at him. Billy looked back down at the activity below, and without thinking, he vaulted the guardrail, stepped off the ledge and into space.

19.

UNEXPECTED ASSISTANCE

"…and I believe we can now go live to the scene, where our reporter Louise Broadley has some breaking news for us. Louise?"

Nicholas Hunter, the reporter who sat behind the desk for 'News on the Hour,' looked at a large TV screen off to his right. A young woman with short brown hair looked at the camera, her face grave.

"That's right, Nick. We now know that an unidentified team of terrorists have taken control of the Natural History Museum, here in GateHaven. Their intention it seems, is to take for ransom billionaire executive, Darius Crane.

"The museum was closed to the general public today,

except for the class of children from Prince John's school, who were guests of Mr. Crane himself."

"And what of the miracle escape of a schoolboy from the roof of the museum just a few hours ago?"

"What we do know is that he is fine, and is being questioned by the police as we speak. For those of you who have just joined us, a pupil somehow managed to evade capture and make his way up to the roof, where he jumped before the terrorists could grab him. Fortunately the boy did not have far to fall, as there was already a fire fighter's ladder being raised to lift him to safety.

"Spectators who witnessed the leap for freedom said the boy is lucky to be alive, and that's down to the expertise of the GateHaven Fire Brigade. With the boy helping the authorities with enquiries, and the terrorists keeping quiet, all we can do is play the waiting game. This is Louise Broadley for News on the Hour, here at GateHaven Natural History Museum."

"I thought you said all the kids were accounted for," one of the kidnappers said addressing Mr. Lamb. There was a sudden muttering among the school kids sat huddled together on the carpeted floor. Jen's face was white with fear.

"I must have miscounted," Mr. Lamb replied in a croaky voice.

"'Miscounted?'" the masked man spat. "What kind of teacher are you when you can't even do a simple head count?"

Suddenly, the masked man's hand whipped out and caught Mr. Lamb with a vicious backhand across the face. The teacher staggered back from the blow. There was a long pause, as the masked man stared at Mr. Lamb. Then slowly he raised a hand and pointed.

"What's wrong with your face?"

Instead of a red mark where he had been slapped, the skin seemed distorted, creased, like crumpled cloth. Mr. Lamb raised a hand to his cheek and froze as he felt the damage there.

"You're wearing some sort of ma-"

Moving swifter than a man of his advancing years was able; Mr. Lamb drove the palm of his left hand up under the chin of the masked man. The force of the blow lifted him clean off his feet. Lamb reached into his briefcase and drew out a small black disc.

He threw it onto the floor just as the other masked men were raising their weapons. There was a flash of intense light followed by a deafening bang, disorienting everyone in the room, except for Mr. Lamb, who had been expecting it. The sound of hurried movement was everywhere, followed by grunts of pain.

Then all was quiet again, save for the muffled sobbing of some of the children. Blake raised his head, blinking through the flashing strobes of light. In the last twenty seconds, things in the room had taken a dramatic turn. All of their captors had been somehow incapacitated. They lay sprawled around the room, tied up and unconscious.

"How did you manage…" but the words caught in Miles' throat as he looked at Lamb's ruined face.

The skin hung in strips, the features badly distorted. Mr. Lamb reached up and ripped his face away. Blake watched in horror as it fluttered to the floor like a tattered flag. With amazing swiftness, 'Mr. Lamb' had whipped out a black mask and was already pulling it over his real face. Two opaque one-way eye lenses stared unblinkingly at the curator.

"Just who are you?" Miles asked, dazed. Some of the girls were crying again. "Where's the real Mr. Lamb?"

"I took his place," was the honest reply as the masked man removed the rest of his clothing to reveal a sleek black body suit beneath. "Don't worry about him; he'll have nothing more than a headache when he wakes up."

He reached into his briefcase and pulled out gloves and boots. He slipped these on, and the transformation from Mr. Lamb was complete.

"Who are you?"

"Wade. Believe it or not, I'm on your side."

"What are you going to do?" Miles asked, still not knowing whether this stranger could be trusted.

"I've got to stop these thugs before it gets out of hand. I know it's difficult but you're going to have to trust me. Just stay here and keep an eye on the kids and I'll do the rest."

"I don't even know if my son is all right," Miles said

suddenly in a worried voice.

"He's fine," Wade said as he looked at the skylight overhead.

"How do you know?" Miles asked, following the man's gaze.

Wade tapped the side of his mask. "I've been listening to the police band all afternoon. Brave lad you've got there, going for help like that."

"I'll give him brave when I get my hands on him," Miles said, though he wasn't kidding anyone. The relief in his voice was obvious.

From the middle of the room, Jen overheard the news about Billy, and grinned despite herself.

"I need to get out of this room," Wade said, "and I need to do it as quietly as possible. Any suggestions?"

"I wouldn't go that way," Miles replied, still looking up at the skylight, "they would have activated the alarms,"

"That's what I thought. What about the door?"

"My pass key will open it," Blake said, though he looked nervous. "What if there's a guard outside?"

"There isn't. What with all the goons in here there

would be no need, and with the rooms being soundproofed, no one heard us."

Together, the two men approached the door. Blake reached into his pocket and drew out a key card.

"You sure about this?" he asked Wade. When the man nodded wordlessly, Blake swiped the card through a slot by the door. A green light flashed on the keypad and he punched in a code. The security door began to rise.

"Close it when I'm gone," Wade said as he peered out into the corridor.

"What about the men in here? Won't they wake up?"

"They're not going anywhere." Wade stepped out into the hall. "Okay, now shut this door behind me."

Blake nodded, and moments later the door was sliding back in place. Wade reached for his belt buckle and pressed a small stud concealed there. For a second nothing happened, and then electrical energy surged through the suit's circuitry. There was a brief flicker, and Wade vanished!

The suit was equipped with a light emitting polymer

membrane which when activated, would duplicate on the front of the costume what was behind it. As long as Wade stuck close to a wall and moved slowly, he was invisible.

The suit had saved his life only last night in the hangar. Tied to the chair, Crane's goons had thought Wade helpless. As they approached, Wade had managed to scuff one of his boots loose. He pushed back, knocking the chair over so that he was on his back staring up at the light overhead.

Wade took aim and kicked the loosened boot into the air. It hit the light bulb. Under the cover of darkness, he activated the suit's chameleon circuits using the special button hidden in the palm of his left glove, a secondary back up in case he could not reach his belt. The approaching goons switched on their torches and shone them to where Wade should have been lying.

They did what Wade had hoped, and panicked. If they had taken the time, they would have noticed Wade's bare foot and face, seeing As how he had kicked his boot off and his mask had been removed. However, all they saw was an empty chair. Together they ran for the door at the far end of the hangar to raise the alarm, but they were too late. Wade had already worked himself free of the cuffs.

They never made it to the door.

Wade made straight for GateHaven. It was simplicity itself to find out about the school trip that Monday, just by monitoring the calls in and out of the museum. What was slightly more difficult was taking Mr. Lamb's place. Wade had entered Lamb's house that evening and drugged the teacher with a sleeping dart. The rest of the night had been spent duplicating Lamb's face.

And here he was. He walked slowly along the carpeted hallway, not making a sound. There were four guards in the foyer, two behind the main desk, and two covering the main entrance.

A closer inspection of the main doors showed Wade that they were booby-trapped. He sidled forward to the main desk, careful to keep close to the wall. He edged around and in behind the guards without detection.

Reaching carefully into a compartment in his belt, Wade withdrew a gun, no bigger than the palm of his hand. He took careful aim and shot the first man in the back of the neck with a sleeping dart. He slumped forward immediately, the second guard following him in rapid succession.

Just then, a small alarm sounded in the circuitry of Wade's mask, quiet enough so that only he could hear it. It meant that the battery life of the chameleon circuits was all but depleted. He had less than five minutes before the system would shut itself down for recharging. In other words, he would be visible again.

Two more guards remained in the foyer. The struggle was brief. He secured the unconscious men with nylon ties to the wrists and ankles, just as the batteries died and he flickered into view.

Wade vaulted the reception desk and headed for the stairs to the first floor. As he sprinted across the tiled floor, he caught movement down the corridor leading to the central exhibition hall.

Darius Crane was striding toward him. Over his shoulder was the unconscious form of Kyle McKinley. Bizarrely, the boy had a steel pipe wrapped around him. In Crane's free hand was a large ancient looking mallet.

Crane was seemingly oblivious to Wade. Then he looked up, stopped and blinked at the masked man before him. Realization of who he was looking at sunk in.

"What do I have to do to be rid of you, Mr. Wade?" the billionaire grimaced.

"Hey, I can't help it if I'm persistent."

It happened before Wade could even move. A hurricane wind rose from nowhere, blasting the length of the hallway and into the foyer. Wade was swept off his feet. The winds scattered objects and furniture before it, swallowing it all up like some ravenous beast. The pterodon skeleton swayed for a moment as if alive, and then disintegrated into a hundred pieces. All of the debris headed for the main door.

"NO," Crane roared, realizing his mistake. Bookcases, plant stands, carpeting, the odd dinosaur skeleton, and an adventurer who went by the name of Wade, went crashing into the protective screening across the glass frontage of the Gate Haven museum.

The noise of the explosion was deafening. The support pillars at the front of the building blew outwards. Dust, glass and plaster rained down everywhere. Screams for the crowd to get back rang through the curtain of billowing dust. There followed an ominous cracking sound from high up, as the upper frontage of the five floor building came crashing down onto the front steps.

Outside, Billy Blake stepped out of the back of an ambulance and wondered if anyone in the museum was still alive.

20.

A SPOT OF BAD WEATHER

This was all Wade's fault. Still, Crane thought as he looked at the remains of the foyer, Wade was out of his hair forever. Placing Kyle on the floor, Crane took a closer look. Most of the lights were gone but he could still see well enough to find his way over to the remains of the desk. On the floor behind it were two of his men, trussed up like Christmas turkeys.

A mobile phone rang from somewhere on the floor, and Crane picked through the rubble, finally locating it.

"Yes?" Crane said into it.

"Station one, what the hell is going on down there?" a rattled voice said on the other end.

"This is Crane. Who is this?"

"Sir?" There was a brief pause. "This is Cook on the third floor. Are you all right? It sounds like World War III down there!"

"Have you left your post?" Crane barked.

"No Sir," Cook replied. "Instructions were to stay at our stations regardless of what was happening on the lower floors."

"Have you been in touch with anyone else?"

"Markey on the second floor, and Palmer on the fifth. I can't raise Hannis on the first floor."

"Contact the police outside and tell them the explosion was a demonstration of how serious we are. Tell them we expect the helicopter on the roof at the specified time. Is that understood?"

"Yes Sir."

"Good man. Now get on with it."

Crane slipped the phone into his pocket. Everything was still on schedule. He turned and headed back to where he had left McKinley. As he rounded the corner, McKinley was gone. In his place lay the twisted steel pipe. Crane took out the phone and dialled Cook on the third floor.

"There's something else I need you to do for me," he said in a barely restrained tone. "There's a kid roaming the corridors. I want him detained. Shoot him if you have to, but keep him alive."

He was operating on instinct. It had taken a supreme effort to free himself from the pipe and get away. The safest place he could think of was the roof. Once up there his strength would return and he could leap to another roof to get away.

Then he thought of his classmates held captive. He could not leave them here. Many of the exhibition halls had skylights. If he could make it to the roof, he could find where they were being kept.

Gritting his teeth against his aching muscles Kyle took the stairs three at a time, barrelling through the swing doors at the top and into the fifth floor corridor beyond.

"Stop!" he heard someone yell in a commanding

tone. Kyle saw two men bearing down on him with guns drawn. Turning on his heel to head back the way he came, Kyle was brought up short as a hail of bullets ripped up the carpet at his feet. The boy yelled and stumbled back as another volley smacked into the wall mere inches from his head. Kyle was so scared that he froze on the spot.

"Okay Sonny-Jim, don't move a muscle. Mr Crane's been looking for you. Don't make any false moves or I'll put a bullet in your leg."

Kyle could hear the words but none of them was making sense to him. Someone had just shot at him.

With a gun.

A really big gun.

He looked through unfocussed eyes at the two men advancing. He could have been killed was the only thought rolling over in his head. Fear had rooted him in place, just as it had before when he had surprised those two car thieves.

Billy would know what to do. He was scrabbling through those air ducts going for help. He didn't have super strength but it hadn't stopped him.

Boiling anger suddenly welled up in him. Anger directed at himself, at his treatment of Billy. A red mist dropped before his eyes. He didn't know how to punish himself, so he did the next best thing and redirected his hatred of himself at the men before him now. In that instant, all fear was gone. Something else seemed to take over as Kyle dropped to his knees.

The men aimed their weapons and prepared to fire. In the blink of an eye, Kyle grabbed two handfuls of carpeting that ran the length of the corridor and ripped it from the floor as easily as if he was removing a sticking plaster from a cut.

The men were thrown off their feet as the floor literally moved under them. They landed with a grunt of pain, and Kyle was on them before they could gather their wits. Two blows to the chin rendered the men unconscious.

Kyle picked up their guns and crushed them. A door at the end of the corridor banged open. He turned in time to see another of Crane's goons coming at him, weapon drawn. The gun spat hot lead at the teenager, and if Kyle hadn't moved in time, it would have cut him in half.

Diving forward into a roll, Kyle came up right in front of his attacker. He didn't hold back.

Kyle punched him hard in the chest, the force of the blow sending the man back the way he came. He hit the doors hard, crumpling to the floor. Kyle crept out onto the landing and chanced a look over the railing at the stairs below. Three more men were headed his way.

Allowing them to reach the landing directly below him, Kyle leapt over railing and dropped one floor, landing directly on top of one of them, flattening him in an instant. So taken by surprise were the other two that they didn't have time to react. Kyle leapt upon the one, punching him in the side of the head, while at the same time lashing out with his foot and catching the other in the belly.

The last one dropped to his knees gasping for breath. Kyle grabbed the front of his uniform, pulled him to his feet, and spun him face first into the wall. He joined his colleagues at Kyle's feet.

He tied the men up with strips of their uniforms and returned to the fifth floor. He'd just taken out six of

Crane's men! How many were left?

Then something hurtled the length of the corridor directly at him. He twisted aside in time as the missile streaked past him. It had been so close that Kyle felt his hair lift as it passed.

A now familiar weakness took hold of him, and he turned to see Darius Crane at the other end of the corridor, hand outstretched. Kyle heard a noise from the other end of the corridor. As fantastic as it sounded, the hammer was pulling itself out of the wall it was embedded.

The hammer was trying to return to Crane's hand. It streaked back along the corridor, and Kyle, for reasons he didn't really know stretched out a hand as it passed him and caught the handle! The teenager was ripped off his feet, and only his strength prevented his arm from being dislocated.

The hammer suddenly veered off to one side, ploughing through the wall and into the room beyond, dragging Kyle with it. He must have blacked out for a moment, for Kyle was brought back to his senses by a bellow of rage from somewhere out in the corridor. Kyle was lying on top of the hammer. He could feel the heat of it, almost like a living thing.

The wall beyond exploded. Crane stepped through, looking madder than ever. The billionaire stretched out his gloved hand and Kyle felt the hammer stir beneath him.

Once again, before he knew what he was about, Kyle took hold of the hammer and hurled it with all his might away from Crane. Crane looked as if his eyes might burst from his head as he advanced on the shaken student.

Far from feeling cowed by the madman towering over him, Kyle leapt at Crane with a renewed fury born of desperation. Kyle swung a punch that lifted Crane off his feet sending him sailing back through the hole he had just stepped. Kyle took off after the hammer.

He found it in the next room buried deep in the wall. Kyle reached forward and pulled it from the wall with little effort. The hammer suddenly twisted violently and then flew from his hand before he could tighten his grip.

It streaked across the room and into the outstretched hand of Crane. He wasted no time in sending a blast of electrical energy at Kyle, but the boy was already moving, sprinting toward the large window at the back of the hall.

The room suddenly flipped end over end, and Kyle lost all sense of direction. Not successful with the lightning strikes, Crane filled the entire room with a force ten gale.

Objects in the room were blown around as effortlessly as Kyle was, and he found himself colliding with cabinets, pictures and figurines from whatever exhibition this hall was displaying. He slammed into a wall, into the ceiling, and finally down onto the hard wooden floor, the tiling splintered with the impact. Kyle was left dazed, disoriented and sick to his stomach. He started to rise but was hit square in the chest by a concentrated blast of wind.

Kyle looked up into Crane's cold eyes, and something dawned on him. Crane was struggling. Despite his bravado earlier, Crane looked like he was fighting the hammer for control. In that moment, Kyle had an idea.

With what little strength remained, Kyle forced himself to his feet and before Crane could react, he leapt at him. Kyle grabbed the hammer, wrapping his hands over Crane's. There was a shuddering as if the hammerhead were going to erupt.

"W-what are you doing?" Crane stammered, eyes going wide.

"You wanted my power," Kyle shouted as another gale force wind arose from nowhere, "well you can choke on it!"

"Let go!" Crane screamed. "It's too much, I can't control it!"

The wind rose higher, battering everything in the room, turning furnishings to match wood, and there in the midst of the maelstrom were two bizarre figures, each struggling as if their very lives depended on it. The strength in Kyle's grip finally gave out and he felt his fingers slip on the handle.

Kyle fell away, spent. The tearing winds picked him up and threw him headlong into a wall. Kyle lay there unable to move, and he could only hold his breath against the scene unfolding before his unbelieving eyes.

Darius Crane was on fire.

The man seemed lit up from inside. His mouth stretched in a silent scream, and an unearthly light poured out. Rain started spattering the room, beating down harder by the second, stinging Kyle's face. An almighty cracking sound filled the remains of the hall, and Kyle realised the four walls were beginning to buckle.

Crane's body twitched spasmodically as the full power of the hammer was unleashed. The walls disintegrated as the storm spread out into the corridors and other rooms beyond. Kyle went end over end down the corridor, unable to put up any fight against this force of nature unleashed. The rain had turned to hail; the balls of ice were the size of golf balls as they smashed all the glass in the vicinity.

All the while, the storm was growing geometrically. There was a loud groaning, and for a moment, Kyle thought it was another crash of thunder. Then he looked up and gasped as the ceiling, and then the very roof ruptured like a burst balloon as the storm spilled out into the night sky.

Almost half the roof was gone and the storm was growing proportionately now it had joined the outer atmosphere. The museum was starting to shake under the storm's ferocity. Everywhere was soaked through with rain, and depending on the consistency of the ever-changing weather patterns, parts of the building were starting to freeze.

Kyle could see Crane. The only thing that had changed was the look of terror on his face. The two of them locked eyes. The billionaire was pleading for help

The direct approach to Crane was next to impossible. The winds held him at bay. He needed to get closer, into the calm eye of the storm. Kyle punched his hand into the wooden flooring to anchor himself. He punched into the floorboards with his free hand. There was a loud cracking as the floor splintered. He punched repeatedly, thinking of nothing else but pounding the floor. His hands were bleeding but he kept up the rhythmic beating until a ragged hole started to appear underneath him.

Finally, his right hand went through and felt no resistance. Kyle reached into the hole with both hands and wrenched the floor apart. He was through in an instant. He fell into the corridor directly below the fifth floor corridor. Kyle paused to get his bearings then walked along the hallway looking at the ceiling as he went. He'd taken no more than twenty steps when he stopped, crouched and jumped for the ceiling.

His bloody fists sank into the plaster and he held firm with his left, while punching with all his might with the right. Ceiling tiles, plaster, wood and insulation rained down on him, but Kyle didn't let up until he punched through to clear air again. Grabbing the outer edges of the ragged hole Kyle swung his legs up and kicked through what was left. The kick was strong enough to take him up, through and into the corridor that he'd just left.

He had done it. He was beyond the storm. Kyle leapt at Crane again, but this time he went for the belt. With what strength remained, he pulled at the buckle, even as he felt his power ebbing. Everything grew dark as Kyle fought to remain conscious; his only thought to destroy the belt at Crane's waist.

There was an almighty flash and Kyle was thrown the length of the hall. He hit the far wall, and for a while, he knew no more.

21.

AFTERMATH

The darkness was an eternity of nothingness. He swam in it, unaware of time or meaning for that matter. It was the voice, coupled with his own growing curiosity that made Kyle open his eyes.

He was flat on his back, staring at the dark sky overhead. Slowly he raised his head, and there, twenty yards away lay Darius Crane. The Billionaire no longer looked like he posed any threat. Kyle picked himself up, and as he did so, he realised he held the Belt of Thor in his hand.

Kyle went over, hardly believing what he was seeing. Crane was badly burned in places, his clothes singed and torn, and his face bloody. His right arm was gone, and so was the glove. There was only a burned stump that ended at the shoulder. The power must have been too great for him, and both his arm and the glove were destroyed in the process.

At Crane's side lay the hammer, quiet and still, hardly the weapon of mass destruction it was before. Kyle stooped and picked it up. He felt the warmth once more, and the quiet voice tickled his ear. Kyle tried to listen, but then another voice spoke.

"You bloody fool," Crane croaked from the floor. He looked up at Kyle with something akin to hate in his eyes. "We could have saved this world of ours. If only you had joined me willingly."

"You had a funny way of asking me," Kyle said, crouching down. "You threatened my friends, kidnapped me, and took what wasn't yours."

"Necessary steps to assure success. Look around you, Kyle. Look at the mess this world is in. Warfare, famine, global warming, energy crisis. I could have ended all that with your hammer. That's all I wanted to do, bring order to this chaotic world before we destroy it."

"But you would have been absolute ruler."

"Who better than I to rule," Crane said licking his lips. "I know about power and how to wield it."

"You're wrong," Kyle whispered close to Crane's ear. "Just look at you, and what you've done to yourself. My dad said that power corrupts, and he was right. So don't lecture me on the right and wrongs of all this. The time would have come when the power of this hammer would not have been enough for you. What would you have done then?"

However, there was no answer forthcoming. Crane's eyes were closed again.

There was sudden movement from the doorway at the end of the corridor. Four armed police officers surged through, their automatic weapons already trained on Kyle.

"Drop your weapon and back away from Mr Crane," one of them barked.

Kyle looked down at the hammer.

"I won't tell you again. Drop the weapon and step out

of the shadows."

They could not see his face, and that was all Kyle needed to know. Turning on his heel, he took off along the corridor, heading for the hole in the far wall. Bullets smacked into the plasterwork all around him, but he was a blur, his strength now fully returned.

Kyle was at the hole in moments, and not slowing, he leapt out into the night, across the yawning gap between the museum and the nearest building across the square. He landed heavily on the roof, the hammer having thrown him off balance.

Kyle looked over his shoulder. The officers had reached the hole and were staring open mouthed at his leap for freedom. Before the officers could raise their weapons again, Kyle slipped away.

Five minutes later, Kyle had traversed the rooftops, ending up on the opposite side of the square overlooking the museum. From his high vantage point, it looked like it was all over. The police were escorting Crane's men from the building at gunpoint. They were being frog marched into the back of large black van.

Moments later, Kyle's classmates stumbled out across the fallen masonry, led by fire and paramedic crews. Movement at the edge of his vision made Kyle turn in time to see Billy rushing from the rear doors of an ambulance toward the straggling kids.

A figure detached itself from the throng and ran headlong at Billy, and Kyle saw that it was Jenny Tate. She wrapped Billy in a bone-breaking hug, which Billy returned with enthusiasm. When they finally broke apart both were grinning foolishly at each other. Then Jen punched Billy in the arm and started ranting at him.

Kyle grinned. Billy had obviously taken a great risk to get out, and was now paying the price for it. However, it was about to get worse, for Miles Blake had just stepped into the night, his eyes darting here and there.

He finally spotted his son and made a beeline for him, his face like thunder. Instead of exploding at Billy, he wrapped him up in a huge hug. It was some time before he let him go.

Other parents were pushing their way through the police line, trying to locate their son or daughter, lines of worry etching their faces. There were cries of relief as families were reunited, and watching from on high Kyle forgot his aches and pains for a moment.

This was what had been worth fighting for. Moreover, as Kyle looked on, he realised that if he were to go on trying to help, then his identity would have to be closely guarded. He could not risk anyone threatening those he loved.

As Kyle mulled this over, so his eyes fell on his dad down at street level, and panic rose in Kyle's chest. He had to get back into the museum!

Moving faster than he had ever done before, Kyle hid the hammer and belt in a broken air conditioning unit, and making a mental note as to where he had put them, streaked off across the rooftops, finally leaping back across to the remains of the museum roof.

Kyle looked down into a ruined skylight. The hall below was dark and quiet. Ripping the lock off, Kyle eased the skylight open and dropped inside. Now all he had to do was get past all the police and emergency crews and make it back to the first aid room.

Yeah, that was all.

However, didn't the first aid room have its own skylight? Kyle retraced his steps hurriedly and was back on the roof in moments. He raced across the remains of the rooftop, looking in all the remaining skylights, until finally finding the room he was looking for.

Kyle popped the lock and slipped in. The room was a right mess. Then Kyle caught a sight of himself in the wall mirror and saw that he was no better. Hopefully the state of the room would account for his injuries. Water had seeped under the door and upset everything. He spent a minute making more of a mess, smashing his hands into the ceiling to bring some of it down on him.

Now all Kyle had to do was lie on the floor next to the table he had been lying on,

and wait to be found. He took up the position. He could not wait to see Billy and get his side of the story. There was also the small matter of what he was going to do with the hammer. He would have to retrieve it when everything had calmed down. Maybe Billy could make sense of it all. If Kyle wasn't the one who the hammer was looking for, just who was it?

There was also the matter of Darius Crane. He knew Kyle's secret. How could he keep the man quiet? Question after question rattled its way through his head. All of them went unanswered.

After a couple of minutes, Kyle found his eyes becoming heavy, so he closed them.

There was the sound of people on the other side of the door.

"Get those axes over here, this door's stuck. There might be someone inside."

As he heard the first blow hit the door, an exhausted Kyle fell asleep under the table. It had, after all been a very busy night.

22.

Endings & Beginnings.

The double doors to the emergency ward banged open, and in rushed the most beautiful woman the doctor had ever seen. Her shoulder length platinum blonde hair flew behind her as stiletto-heeled shoes click-clacked a rapid staccato on the polished floor.

She spotted the doctor and made straight for him.

"I got here as fast as my private jet would allow. Please doctor… my husband… will he…?" She broke off, her lip quivering, the deep green eyes swimming with tears.

"He was admitted to us four hours ago," the doctor said, placing a reassuring hand on her shoulder. "It was touch and go for a while, Mrs Crane. His system has received severe trauma. However, we have him stabilized now. What those terrorists subjected him to must have been staggering."

"What's his condition?" Mrs Crane asked, wiping tears away with the back of her hand.

"Well, he has third degree burns to twenty percent of his body, and has lost the sight in his right eye. His right arm is gone too. How this happened is beyond me, but fortunately for him the wound was cauterized, minimising blood loss. However, trauma of this scale has put Mr Crane into a coma."

Mrs Crane blanched. "A coma? For how long?"

The doctor frowned. "It's difficult to say. For now, we're doing all we can."

"May I see him?" Mrs Crane asked.

"Of course, but please keep it brief."

She nodded. As she moved to enter the room, the doctor spoke again.

"There was one thing though."

She turned. "Yes?"

"Your husband, he came around very briefly. He spoke

a word, well a name actually. 'McKinley.' Does that name mean anything to you?"

Julia Crane paused at the door. "No," she replied. And with that, she entered the room, closing the door behind her.

Lightning Source UK Ltd.
Milton Keynes UK
25 March 2010

151871UK00001B/6/P